Flandry
Wondered
if he'd
LOST HIS MIND...

The old records said the planet was barren, always had been, always would be. But suddenly, from behind boulders and ice banks, the grotesque bugs came soaring toward him. Thirty centimeters long, they had ten claw-footed legs each, a tail ending in twin spikes, a head on which half a dozen antennae moved.

Two landed on his helmet. He heard the clicks, felt the astonishing impact. Looking down, he saw others at his waist, clinging to his legs, swarming around his boots. Jaws champed, claws dug. They found the joints in his armor and went to work.

Other SIGNET Science Fiction Titles
You Will Enjoy

A Circus
of Hells

by
POUL ANDERSON

A SIGNET BOOK from
NEW AMERICAN LIBRARY
TIMES MIRROR

Ø SIGNET TRADEMARK REG. U.S. PAT. OFF. AND FOREIGN COUNTRIES
REGISTERED TRADEMARK—MARCA REGISTRADA
HECHO EN CHICAGO, U.S.A.

SIGNET, SIGNET CLASSICS, MENTOR AND PLUME BOOKS
are published by The New American Library, Inc.,
1301 Avenue of the Americas, New York, New York 10019

FIRST PRINTING, MAY, 1970

PRINTED IN THE UNITED STATES OF AMERICA

This book thanks William R. Johnson, wherever he is nowadays, for several excellent ideas about Talwin which he contributed, and will gladly stand him a drink any time it can get together with him.

CHAPTER

I

The story is of a lost treasure guarded by curious monsters, and of captivity in a wilderness, and of a chase through reefs and shoals that could wreck a ship. There is a beautiful girl in it, a magician, a spy or two, and the rivalry of empires. So of course—Flandry was later tempted to say—it begins with a coincidence.

However, the likelihood that he would meet Tachwyr the Dark was not fantastically low. They were in the same profession, which had them moving through a number of the same places; and they also shared the adventurousness of youth. To be sure, once imperialism is practiced on an interstellar scale, navies grow in size until the odds are huge against any given pair of their members happening on each other. Nevertheless, many such encounters were taking place, as was inevitable on one of the rare occasions when a Merseian warship visited a Terran planet. A life which included *no* improbable events would be the real statistical impossibility.

The planet was Irumclaw, some 200 light-years from Sol in that march of the human realm which faced Betelgeuse. Lieutenant (j.g.) Dominic Flandry had been posted there not long before, with much wailing and gnashing of teeth until he learned that even so dismal a clod had its compensations. The Merseian vessel was the cruiser *Brythioch*, on a swing through the buffer region of unclaimed, mostly unknown suns between the spaces ruled in the names of Emperor and Roidhun. Neither government would have allowed any craft belonging to its rival, capable of spouting nuclear fire, any appreciable distance into its territory. But border authorities could, at discretion, accept a "goodwill visit." It broke the monotony and gave a slight hope of observing the kind of trivia which, fitted together, now and then revealed a fact the opposition would have preferred to keep secret.

In this case Merseia profited, at least initially.

Official hospitality was exchanged. Besides protocol, the humans were motivated, whether they knew it or not, to

7

enjoy the delicate *frisson* that came from holding converse with those who—beneath every diplomatic phrase—were the enemy. Flandry did know it; he had seen more of life than the average twenty-one-year-old. He was sure the liberty parties down in Old Town were being offered quite a few drinks, and other amenities in certain cases.

Well, why not? They had been long in the deeps between the stars. If they went straight back from here, they must travel a good 140 light-years—about ten standard days at top hyperspeed, but still an abyss whose immensity and strangeness wore down the hardiest spirit—before they could raise the outermost of the worlds they called their own. They needed a few hours of small-scale living, be their hosts never so hostile.

Which we aren't anyway, Flandry thought. *We should be, but we aren't, most of us.* He grinned. *Including me.*

Though he would have liked to join the fun, he couldn't. The junior officers of Irumclaw Base must hold the customary reception for their opposite numbers from the ship. (Their seniors gave another in a separate building. The Merseians, variously bemused or amused by the rigid Terran concept of rank, conformed. They set more store by ceremony and tradition, even that of aliens, than latter-day humans did.) While some of the visitors spoke Anglic, it turned out that Flandry was the only man on this planet who knew Eriau. The mess hall had no connection to the linguistic computer and there was no time to jury-rig one. His translations would be needed more than his physical presence.

Not that the latter was any disgrace, he reflected rather smugly. He was tall and lithe and wore his dress uniform with panache and had become a favorite among the girls downhill. Despite this, he remained well liked by the younger men, if not always by his superiors.

He entered at the appointed evening hour. Under Commander Abdullah's fishy eye, he saluted the Emperor's portrait not with his usual vague wave but with a snap that well-nigh dislocated his shoulder. *And a heel click to boot,* he reminded himself. Several persons being in line ahead of him, he had a minute for taking stock.

Its tables removed except for one bearing refreshments —and its chairs, in deference to the guests—the room stretched dreary. Pictures of former personnel, trophies and citations for former accomplishments, seemed to make its walls just the more depressing. An animation showed a park on Terra, trees nodding, in the background the skyward leap of a rich family's residential tower and airborne vehicles glittering like diamond dust; but it reminded him too well of how far he was from those dear comforts. He preferred the darkness in the real window. It was open and a breeze gusted through, warm, laden with unearthly odors.

The Merseians were a more welcome sight, if only as proof that a universe did exist beyond Irumclaw. Forty of them stood in a row, enduring repeated introductions with the stoicism appropriate to a warrior race.

They resembled especially large men . . . somewhat. A number of their faces might have been called good-looking in a craggy fashion; their hands each had four fingers and a thumb; the proportions and articulations of most body parts were fairly anthropoid. But the posture was forward-leaning, balanced by a heavy tail. The feet, revealed by sandals, were splayed, webbed, and clawed. The skin was hairless and looked faintly scaled; depending on subspecies, its color ranged from the pale green which was commonest through golden brown to ebony. The head had two convoluted bony orifices where man's has external ears. A ridge of serrations ran from its top, down the spine to the end of the tail.

Most of this anatomy was concealed by their uniforms: baggy tunic, snug breeches, black with silver trim and insignia. The latter showed family connections and status as well as rank and service. The Merseians had politely disarmed themselves, in that none carried a pistol at his wide belt; the Terrans, in turn, had refrained from asking them to remove their great knuckleduster-handled war knives.

It wasn't the differences between them and men that caused trouble, Flandry knew. It was the similarities—in planets of origin and thus in planets desired; in the energy of warm-blooded animals, the instincts of ancestors who hunted, the legacies of pride and war—

"*Afal* Ymen, may I present Lieutenant Flandry," Abdullah intoned. The young man bowed to the huge form, whose owner corresponded approximately to a commander, and received a nod of the ridged and shining pate. He proceeded, exchanging names and bows with every subordinate Merseian and wondering, as they doubtless did too, when the farce would end and the drinking begin.

"Lieutenant Flandry."

"*Mei* Tachwyr."

They stopped, and stared, and both mouths fell open.

Flandry recovered first, perhaps because he became aware that he was holding up the parade. "Uh, this is a, uh, pleasant surprise," he stammered in Anglic. More of his wits returned. He made a formal Eriau salutation: "Greeting and good fortune to you, Tachwyr of the Vach Rueth."

"And . . . may you be in health and strength, Dominic Flandry . . . of Terra," the Merseian replied.

For another moment their eyes clashed, black against gray, before the man continued down the line.

After a while he got over his astonishment. Albeit unexpected, the happenstance that he and Tachwyr had met again did not look especially important. Nonetheless, he went robotlike through the motions of sociability and of being an interpreter. His gaze and mind kept straying toward his former acquaintance. And Tachwyr himself was too young to mask entirely the fact that he was as anxious to get together with Flandry.

Their chance came in a couple of hours, when they managed to dodge out of their respective groups and seek the refreshment table. Flandry gestured. "May I pour for you?" he asked. "I fear that except for the telloch, we've run out of things native to your planet."

"I regret to say you have been had," Tachwyr answered. "It is a dreadful brand. But I like your—what is it called? —skoksh?"

"That makes two of us." Flandry filled glasses for them. He had already had several whiskies and would have preferred this one over ice. However, he wasn't about to look sissified in front of a Merseian.

"Ah . . . cheers," Tachwyr said, lifting his tumbler. His throat and palate gave the Anglic word an accent for which there were no Anglic words.

Flandry could form Merseian speech better if not perfectly. *"Tor ychwei."* With both hands he extended his glass so that the other might take the first sip.

Tachwyr followed it with half of his own in a single gulp. *"Arrach!"* Relaxed a little, he cocked his head and smiled; but under the shelf of brow ridge, his glance held very steady on the human. "Well," he said, "what brings you here?"

"I was assigned. For a Terran year, worse luck. And you?"

"The same, to my present ship. I see you are now in the Intelligence Corps."

"Like yourself."

Tachwyr the Dark—his skin was a slightly deeper green than is usual around the Wilwidh Ocean—could not altogether suppress a scowl. "I started in that branch," he said.

10

"You were a flyer when you came to Merseia." He paused. "Were you not?"

"Oh, yes," Flandry said. "I transferred later."

"At Commander Abrams' instigation?"

Flandry nodded. "Mostly. He's a captain now, by the way."

"So I have heard. We . . . take an interest in him."

After the Starkad affair, Flandry thought, *you would. Between us, Max Abrams and I wrecked a scheme concocted by none less than Brechdan Ironrede, Protector of the Roidhun's Grand Council.*

How much do you know about that, Tachwyr? You were only put to showing me around and trying to pump me, when Abrams and I were on your world as part of the Hauksberg misson. And the truth about Starkad was never made public; no one concerned could afford to let it come out.

You do remember us, though, Tachwyr. If nothing else, you must have gathered that we were instrumental in causing Merseia quite a bit of trouble. It bothers you to have found me here.

Better get off the subject. "You remain through tomorrow? I admit Irumclaw has less to offer than Merseia, but I'd like to return part of the courtesy you gave me."

Again Tachwyr was slow to speak. "Thank you, negative. I have already arranged to tour the area with shipmates." The Eriau phrasing implied a commitment which no honorable male would break.

Flandry reflected that a male would not ordinarily bind himself so strongly to something so minor.

What the devil? the human thought. *Maybe they aim to sample our well-known Terran decadence and he doesn't want me to realize their well-known Merseian virtue can slack off that much.* "Stay in a party," he warned. "Some of those bars are almost as dangerous as the stuff they serve."

Tachwyr uttered the throaty laugh of his species, settled down on the tripod of feet and tail, and started yarning. Flandry matched him. They enjoyed themselves until the man was called away to interpret a tedious conversation between two engineer officers.

CHAPTER

II

Such was the prologue. He had practically forgotten it when the adventure began. That was on a certain night about eight months later.

Soon after the red-orange sun had set, he left the naval compound and walked downhill. No one paid him any heed. A former commandant had tried to discourage his young men from seeking the occasionally lethal corruptions of Old Town. He had declared a large part of it off limits. Meeting considerable of the expense out of his own pocket, he had started an on-base recreation center which was to include facilities for sports, arts, and crafts, as well as honest gambling and medically certified girls. But the bosses below knew how to use money and influence. The commandant was transferred to a still more bleak and insignificant outpost. His successor dismantled what had been built, informed the men jovially that what they did off duty was their business, and was said to be drawing a nice extra income.

Flandry sauntered in elegance. The comet gleaming on either shoulder was so new that you might have looked for diffidence from him. But his bonnet was tilted more rakishly on his seal-brown hair than a strict interpretation of rules would have allowed; his frame was draped in a fantastic glittergold version of dress tunic and snowy trousers tucked into handmade beefleather half-boots; the cloak that fluttered behind him glowed with phosphorescent patterns through the chill dusk; and while he strolled, he sang a folk ballad concerning the improbable adventures of a Highland tinker.

It made a good cover for the fact that he was not out for pleasure.

Beyond the compound walls, the homes of the wealthy loomed amidst grandly downsweeping private parks. In a way, Flandry thought, they epitomized man's trajectory. Once the settlement had been sufficiently large and prosperous, and sufficiently within the Imperial sphere, to attract not only merchants but aristocrats. Old Town had bustled with culture as well as commerce—provincial, no doubt, this far from Terra; nevertheless, live and genuine, worthy of the respectful emulation of the autochthons.

Tonight Irumclaw lay like a piece of wreckage at the edge of the receding tide of empire. What mansions were not standing hollow had become the property of oafs, and showed it. (The oafs were not to be scoffed at. Several of them directed large organizations devoted to preying on the spacemen who visited and the Navy men who guarded what transshipment facilities remained in use.) Outside the treaty port boundaries, barbarism rolled forward as the natives abandoned civilization with a perhaps justifiable contempt.

Past the residential section, workshops and warehouses hulked black in the night, and Flandry moved alert with a hand near the needle gun under his tunic. Robberies and murders had happened here. Lacking the police to clean out this area, assuming he wanted to, the commandant had settled for advising men on liberty not to go through alone.

Flandry had been shocked to learn that when he first arrived. "We could do it ourselves—establish regular patrols —if he'd order it. Doesn't he care? What kind of chief is he?"

His protest had been delivered in private to another scout, Lieutenant Commander Eisenschmitt. The latter, having been around for a while, shrugged. "The kind that any place like this gets," he answered. "We don't rate attention at GHQ, so naturally we're sent the hacks, boobs, and petty crooks. Good senior officers are too badly needed elsewhere. When Irumclaw does get one it's an accident, and he doesn't stay long."

"Damn it, man, we're on the border!" Flandry pointed out the window of the room where they sat. It had been dark then, too. Betelgeuse glowed bloody-brilliant among the hosts of stars where no writ ran. "Beyond there—Merseia!"

"Yeh. And the gatortails expanding in all directions except when we bar the way. I know. But this is the far edge of nowhere . . . in the eyes of an Imperial government that can't see past its perfume-sniffing nose. You're fresh from Terra, Dom. You ought to understand better than me. I expect we'll pull out of Irumclaw entirely inside another generation."

"No! Can't be! Why, that'd leave this whole flank exposed for six parsecs inward. We'd have no way of pro-

13

tecting its commerce . . . of, of staying around in any force—"

"Uh-huh." Eisenschmitt nodded. "On the other hand, the local commerce isn't too profitable any more, less each year. And think of the saving to the Imperial treasury if we end operations. The Emperor should be able to build a dozen new palaces complete with harems."

Flandry had not been able to agree at the time. He was too lately out of a fighting unit and a subsequent school where competence was demanded. Over the months, though, he saw things for himself and drew his own sad conclusions.

There were times when he would have welcomed a set-to with a bandit. But it had not befallen, nor did it on this errand into Old Town.

The district grew around him, crumbling buildings left over from pioneer days, many of them simply the original beehive-shaped adobes of the natives slightly remodeled for other life forms. Streets and alleys twisted about under flimmering glowsigns. Traffic was mainly pedestrian, but noise beat on the eardrums, clatter, shuffle, clop, clangor, raucous attempts at music, a hundred different languages, once in a while a muffled scream or a bellow of rage. The smells were equally strong, body odors, garbage, smoke, incense, dope. Humans predominated, but many autochthons were present and space travelers of numerous different breeds circulated among them.

Outside a particular joyhouse, otherwise undistinguished from the rest, an Irumclavian used a vocalizer to chant in Anglic: "Come one, come all, come in, no cover, no minimum. Every type of amusement, pleasure, and thrill. No game too exotic, no stakes too high or low. Continuous sophisticated entertainment. Delicious food and drink, stimulants, narcotics, hallucinogens, emphasizers, to your order, to your taste, to your purse. Every sex and every technique of seventeen, yes, seventeen intelligent species ready to serve your desires, and this does not count racial, mutational, and biosculp variations. Come one, come all—"
Flandry went in. He chanced to brush against two or three of the creature's arms. The blue integument felt cold in the winter air.

The entrance hall was hot and stuffy. An outsize human in a gaudy uniform said, "Welcome, sir. What is your wish?" while keeping eyes upon him that were like chips of obsidian.

"Are you Lem?" Flandry responded.

"Uh, yeh. And you—?"

14

"I am expected."

"Urh. Take the gravshaft to the top, that's the sixth floor, go left down the hall to a door numbered 666, stand in front of the scan and wait. When it opens, go up the stairs."

"Six-six-six?" murmured Flandry, who had read more than was common in his service. "Is Citizen Ammon a humorist, do you think?"

"No names!" Lem dropped a hand to the stunner at his hip. "On your way, kid."

Flandry obeyed, even to letting himself be frisked and leaving his gun at the checkstand. He was glad when Door 666 admitted him; that was the sado-maso level, and he had glimpsed things.

The office which he entered, and which sealed itself behind him, recalled Terra in its size and opulence and in the animation of a rose garden which graced a wall. Or so it seemed; then he looked closer and saw the shabbiness of the old furnishings, the garishness of the new. No other human save Leon Ammon was present. A Gorzunian mercenary stood like a shaggy statue in one corner. When Flandry turned his back, the being's musky scent continued to remind him that if he didn't behave he could be plucked into small pieces.

"G' evening," said the man behind the desk. He was grossly fat, hairless, sweating, not especially clean, although his scarlet tunic was of the finest. His voice was high and scratchy. "You know who I am, right? Sit down. Cigar? Brandy?"

Flandry accepted everything offered. It was of prime quality too. He said so.

"You'll do better than this if you stick by me," Ammon replied. His smile went no deeper than his lips. "You haven't told about the invitation my man whispered to you the other night?"

"No, sir, of course not."

"Wouldn't bother me if you did. Nothing illegal about inviting a young chap for a drink and a gab. Right? But you could be in trouble yourself. Mighty bad trouble, and not just with your commanding officer."

Flandry had his suspicions about the origin of many of the subjects on the floor below. Consenting adults . . . after brain-channeling and surgical disguise . . . He studied the tip of his cigar. "I don't imagine you'd've asked me here, sir, if you thought I needed threatening," he said.

"No. I like your looks, Dominic," Ammon said. "Have ever since you started coming to Old Town for your fun.

15

A lot of escapades, but organized like military maneuvers, right? You're cool and tough and close-mouthed. I had a check done on your background."

Flandry expanded his suspicions. Various incidents, when he had been leaned on one way or another, began to look like engineered testing of his reactions. "Wasn't much to find out, was there?" he said. "I'm only a j.g., routinely fresh-minted after serving here for two months. Former flyboy, reassigned to Intelligence, sent back to Terra for training in it and then to Irumclaw for scouting duty."

"I can't really compute that," Ammon said. "If they aim to make you a spy, why have you spend a year flitting in and out of this system?"

"I need practice in surveillance, especially of planets that are poorly known. And the no-man's-land yonder needs watching. Our Merseian chums could build an advanced base there, for instance, or start some other kettle boiling, unbeknownst to us, if we didn't keep scoutboats sweeping around." *Maybe they have anyway.*

"Yes, I got that answer before when I asked, and it still sounds to me like a waste of talent. But it got you to Irumclaw, and I did notice you and had you studied. I learned more than stands on any public record, boy. The whole Starkad business pivoted on you."

Shocked, Flandry wondered how deeply the rot had eaten, if the agent of a medium-scale vice boss on a tenth-rate frontier planet could obtain such information.

"Well, your tour'll soon be up," Ammon said. "Precious little to show for it, right? Right. How'd you like to turn a profit before you leave? A mighty nice profit, I promise you." He rubbed his hands. "Mighty nice."

"Depends," Flandry said. If he'd been investigated as thoroughly as it appeared, there was no use in pretending he had private financial resources, or that he didn't require them if he was to advance his career as far as he hoped. "The Imperium has my oath."

"Sure, sure. I wouldn't ask you to do anything against His Majesty. I'm a citizen myself, right? No, I'll tell you exactly what I want done, if you'll keep it confidential."

"It'd doubtless not do me any good to blab, the way you'll tell me."

Ammon giggled. "Right! Right! You're a sharp one, Dominic. Handsome, too," he added exploringly.

"I'll settle for the sharpness now and buy the handsomeness later," Flandry said. As a matter of fact, while he enjoyed being gray-eyed, he considered his face unduly long and thin, and planned to get it remodeled when he could afford the best.

Ammon sighed and returned to business. "All I want is for you to survey a planet for me. You can do it on your next scouting trip. Report back, privately, of course, and it's worth a flat million, in small bills or whatever shape you prefer." He reached into his desk and extracted a packet. "If you take the job, here's a hundred thousand on account."

A million! Ye gods and demons!

Flandry fought to keep his mask. *No enormous fortune, really. But enough for that necessary nest-feathering—the special equipment, the social contacts—no more wretched budgeting of my pleasure on furlough—* A distant part of him noted with approval how cool his tone stayed. "I have to carry out my assignment."

"I know, I know. I'm not asking you to skimp it. I told you I'm a loyal citizen. But if you jogged off your track awhile—it shouldn't cost more than a couple of weeks extra—"

"Cost me my scalp if anyone found out," Flandry said.

Ammon nodded. "That's how I'll know I can trust you to keep quiet. And you'll trust me, because suborning an Imperial officer is a capital offense—anyhow, it usually is when it involves a matter like this, that's not going to get mentioned to the authorities or the tax assessors."

"Why not send your personal vessel to look?"

Ammon laid aside his mannerisms. "I haven't got one. If I hired a civilian, what hold would I have on him? Especially an Old Town type. I'd likely end up with an extra mouth in my throat, once the word got around what's to be had out there. Let's admit it, even on this miserable crudball I'm not so big."

He leaned forward. "I want to become big," he said. It smoldered in eyes and voice; he shook with the intensity of it. "Once I know, from you, that the thing's worthwhile, I'll sink everything I own and can borrow into building up a reliable outfit. We'll work secretly for the first several years, sell through complicated channels, sock away the profits. Then maybe I'll surface, doctor the story, start paying taxes, move to Terra—maybe buy my way to a patent of nobility, maybe go into politics, I don't know, but I'll be *big*. Do you understand?"

Far too well, Flandry thought.

Ammon dabbed at his glistening forehead. "It wouldn't hurt you, having a big friend," he said. "Right?"

17

Associate, please, Flandry thought. *Perhaps that, if I must. Never friend.*

Aloud: "I suppose I could cook my log, record how trouble with the boat caused delay. She's fast but superannuated, and inspections are lackadaisical. But you haven't yet told me, sir, what the bloody dripping hell this is all about."

"I will, I will." Ammon mastered his emotions. "It's a lost treasure, that's what it is. Listen. Five hundred years ago, the Polesotechnic League had a base here. You've heard?"

Flandry, who had similarly tamed his excitement into alertness, nodded wistfully. He would much rather have lived in the high and spacious days of the trader princes, when no distance and no deed looked too vast for man, than in this twilight of empire. "It got clobbered during the Troubles, didn't it?" he said.

"Right. However, a few underground installations survived. Not in good shape. Not safe to go into. Tunnels apt to collapse, full of nightskulks—you know. Now I thought those vaults might be useful for— Never mind. I had them explored. A microfile turned up. It gave the coordinates and galactic orbit of a planetary system out in what's now no-man's-land. Martian Minerals, Inc., was mining one of the worlds. They weren't publicizing the fact; you remember what rivalries got to be like toward the end of the League era. That's the main reason why knowledge of this system was completely lost. But it was quite a place for a while."

"Rich in heavy metals," Flandry pounced.

Ammon blinked. "How did you guess?"

"Nothing else would be worth exploiting by a minerals outfit, at such a distance from the centers of civilization. Yes." A renewed eagerness surged in Flandry. "A young, metal-rich star, corresponding planets, on one of them a robotic base . . . It was robotic, wasn't it? High-grade central computer—consciousness grade, I'll bet—directing machines that prospected, mined, refined, stored, and loaded the ships when they called. Probably manufactured spare parts for them too, and did needful work on them, besides expanding its own facilities. You see, I don't suppose a world with that concentration of violently poisonous elements in its ground would attract people to a manned base. Easier and cheaper in the long run to automate everything."

"Right. Right." Ammon's chins quivered with his nodding. "A moon, actually, of a planet bigger than Jupiter.

18

More massive, that is—a thousand Terras—though the file does say its gravity condensed it to a smaller size. The moon itself, Wayland they named it, Wayland has about three percent the mass of Terra but half the surface pull. It's that dense."

Mean specific gravity circa eleven, Flandry calculated. *Uranium, thorium—probably still some neptunium and plutonium—and osmium, platinum, rare metals simply waiting to be scooped out—my God! My greed!*

From behind his hard-held coolness he drawled: "A million doesn't seem extravagant pay for opening that kind of opportunity to you."

"It's plenty for a look-see," Ammon said. "That's all I want of you, a report on Wayland. I'm taking the risks, not you.

"First off, I'm risking you'll go report our talk, trying for a reward and a quick transfer elsewhere before my people can get to you. Well, I don't think that's a very big risk. You're too ambitious and too used to twisting regulations around to suit yourself. And too smart, I hope. If you think for a minute, you'll see how I could fix it to get any possible charges against me dropped. But maybe I've misjudged you.

"Then, supposing you play true, the place could turn out to be no good. I'll be short a million, for nothing. More than a million, actually. There's the hire of a partner; reliable ones don't come cheap. And supplies for him; and transporting them to a spot where you can pick them and him up after you've taken off; and—oh, no, boy, you consider yourself lucky I'm this generous."

"Wait a minute," Flandry said. "A partner?"

Ammon leered. "You don't think I'd let you travel alone, do you? Really, dear boy! What'd prevent your telling me Wayland's worthless when it isn't, coming back later as a civilian, and 'happening' on it?"

"I presume if I give you a negative report, you'll . . . request . . . I submit to a narcoquiz. And if I didn't report to you at all, you'd know I had found a prize."

"Well, what if you told them you'd gotten off course somehow and found the system by accident? You could hope for a reward. I can tell you you'd be disappointed. Why should the bureaucrats care, when there'd be nothing in it for them but extra work? I'd lay long odds they'd classify your 'discovery' an Imperial secret and forbid you under criminal penalties ever to mention it anywhere. You might guess differently, though. No insult to you, Dominic. I believe in insurance, that's all. Right?

19

"So my agent will ride along, and give you the navigational data after you're safely away in space, and never leave your side till you've returned and told me personally what you found. Afterward, as a witness to your behavior on active duty, a witness who'll testify under hypnoprobe if need be, why, he'll keep on being my insurance against any change of heart you might suffer."

Flandry blew a smoke ring. "As you wish," he conceded. "It'll be pretty cozy, two in a Comet, but I can rig an extra bunk and— Let's discuss this further, shall we? I think I will take the job, if certain conditions can be met."

Ammon would have bristled were he able. The Gorzunian sensed his irritation and growled. "Conditions? From you?"

Flandry waved his cigar. "Nothing unreasonable, sir," he said airily. "For the most part, precautions that I'm sure you will agree are sensible and may already have thought of for yourself. And that agent you mentioned. Not 'he,' please. It could get fatally irritating, living cheek by unwashed jowl with some goon for weeks. I know you can find a capable and at the same time amiable human female. Right? Right."

He had everything he could do to maintain that surface calm. Beneath it, his pulse racketed—and not simply because of the money, the risk, the enjoyment. He had come here on a hunch, doubtless generated by equal parts of curiosity and boredom. He had stayed with the idea that, if the project seemed too hazardous, he could indeed betray Ammon and apply for duty that would keep him beyond range of assassins. Now abruptly a vision was coming to him, hazy, uncertain, and gigantic.

CHAPTER

III

Djana was hard to shock. But when the apartment door
had closed behind her and she saw what waited, her "No!"
broke free as a near scream.

"Do not be alarmed," said the squatting shape. A vocalizer converted the buzzes and whistles from its lower beak
into recognizable Anglic syllables. "You have nothing to
fear and much to gain."

"You—a man called me—"

"A dummy. It is not desirable that Ammon know you
have met me in private, and surely he has put a monitor
onto you."

Djana felt surreptitiously behind her. As expected, the
door did not respond; it had been set to lock itself. She
clutched her large ornamental purse. A stun pistol lay inside. Her past had seen contingencies.

Bracing herself and wetting her lips, she said, "I don't.
Not with xenos—" and in haste, fearing offense might be
taken, "I mean nonhuman sophonts. It isn't right."

"I suspect a large enough sum would change your
mind," the other said. "You have a reputation for avarice.
However, I plan a different kind of proposition." It moved
slowly closer, a lumpy gray body on four thin legs which
brought the head at its middle about level with her waist.
One tentacle sent the single loose garment swirling about
in a sinuous gesture. Another clutched the vocalizer in
boneless fingers. The instrument was being used with considerable skill; it actually achieved an ingratiating note.
"You must know about me in your turn. I am only Rax,
harmless old Rax, the solitary representative of my species
on this world. I assure you my reproductive pattern is sufficiently unlike yours that I find your assumption comical."

Djana eased a bit. She had in fact noticed the creature
during the three years she herself had been on Irumclaw.
A casual inquiry and answer crossed her recollection, yes,
Rax was a dealer in drugs, legal or illegal, from . . .
where was it? Nobody knew or cared. The planet had

some or other unpronounceable name and orbited in distant parts. Probably Rax had had to make a hurried departure for reasons of health, and had drifted about until it stranded at last on this tolerant shore. Such cases were tiresomely common.

And who could remember all the races in the Terran Empire? Nobody: not when its bounds, unclear though they were, defined a rough globe 400 light-years across. That volume contained an estimated four million suns, most with attendants. Maybe half had been visited once or more, by ships which might have picked up incidental native recruits. And the hundred thousand or so worlds which enjoyed a degree of repeated contact with men—often sporadic—and owed a degree of allegiance to the Imperium—often purely nominal—were too many for a brain to keep track of.

Djana's eyes flickered. The apartment was furnished for a human, in abominable taste. He must be the one who had called her. Now he was gone. Though an inner door stood closed, she never doubted she was alone with Rax. Silence pressed on her, no more relieved by dull traffic sounds from outside than the gloom in the windows was by a few street lights. She grew conscious of her own perfume. *Too damn sweet,* she thought.

"Do be seated." Rax edged closer yet, with an awkwardness that suggested weight on its original planet was significantly lower than Irumclaw's 0.96 g. Did it keep a field generator at home . . . if it had any concept akin to "home"?

She drew a long breath, tossed her head so the tresses flew back over her shoulders, and donned a cocky grin. "I've a living to make," she said.

"Yes, yes." Rax's lower left tentacle groped ropily in a pouch and stretched forth holding a bill. "Here. Twice your regular hourly recompense, I am told. You need but listen, and what you hear should point the way to earning very much more."

"We-e-ell . . ." She slipped the money into her purse, found a chair, drew forth a cigarette and inhaled it into lighting. Her visceral sensations she identified as part fear—this must be a scheme against Ammon, who played rough—and part excitement—a chance to make some *real* credit? Maybe enough to quit this wretched hustle for good?

Rax placed itself before her. She had no way of reading expressions on that face.

"I will tell you what information is possessed by those

whom I represent," the vocalizer said. The spoken language, constructed with pronunciation, vocabulary, and grammar in a one-one relationship to Anglic, rose and fell eerily behind the little transponder. "A junior lieutenant, Dominic Flandry, was observed speaking several times in private with Leon Ammon."

Now why should that interest them especially? she wondered, then lost her thought in her concentration on the words.

"Investigation revealed Ammon's people had come upon something in the course of excavating in this vicinity. Its nature is known just to him and a few trusted confidants. We suspect that others who saw were paid to undergo memory erasure anent the matter, except for one presumably stubborn person whose corpse was found in Mother Chickenfoot's Lane. Subsequently you too have been closeted with Ammon and, later, with Flandry."

"Well," Djana said, "he—"

"Pure coincidence is implausible," Rax declared, "especially when he could ill afford you on a junior lieutenant's pay. It is also known that Ammon has quietly purchased certain spacecraft supplies and engaged a disreputable interplanetary ferrier to take them to the outermost member of this system and leave them there at a specific place, in a cave marked by a small radio beacon that will self-activate when a vessel passes near."

Suddenly Djana realized why Skipper Orsini had sought her out and been lavish shortly after his return. Rax's outfit had bribed him.

"I can't imagine what you're getting at," she said. A draft of smoke swirled and bit in her lungs.

"You can," Rax retorted. "Dominic Flandry is a scoutboat pilot. He will soon depart on his next scheduled mission. Ammon must have engaged him to do something extra in the course of it. Since the cargo delivered to Plannet Eight included impellers and similar gear, the job evidently involves study of a world somewhere in the wilderness. Ammon's discovery was therefore, in all probability, an old record of its existence and possible high value. You are to be his observer. Knowing Flandry's predilections, one is not surprised that he should insist on a companion like you. It follows that you two have been getting acquainted, to make certain you can endure being cooped together for weeks in a small boat.

"Orsini will flit you to Eight. Flandry will surreptitiously land there, pick up you and the supplies, and proceed into interstellar space. Returning, you two will reverse the whole process, and meet in Ammon's office to report."

Djana sat still.

"You give away nothing by affirming this," Rax stated. "My organization *knows*. Where is the lost planet? What is its nature?"

"Who are you working for?" Djana asked mutedly.

"That does not concern you." Rax's tone was mild and Djana took no umbrage. The gang lords of Irumclaw were a murderous lot.

"You owe Ammon no allegiance," Rax urged. "Rather, you owe him a disfavor. Since you prefer to operate independently, and thus compete with the houses, you must pay him for his 'protection.'"

Djana sighed. "If it weren't him, it'd be somebody else."

Rax drew forth a sheaf of bills and riffled them with a fine crisp sound. She estimated—holy saints!—ten thousand credits. "This for answering my questions," it said. "Most likely a mere beginning for you."

She thought, while she inhaled raggedly, *If the business looks too dangerous, I can go tell Leon right away and explain I was playing along—of course, this bunch might learn I'd talked and I'd have to skip—* A flick of white fury: *I shouldn't have to skip! Not ever again!*

She built her sentences with care. "Nobody's told me much. You understand they wouldn't, till the last minute. Your ideas are right, but they're about as far along as my own information goes."

"Has Flandry said nothing to you?"

She plunged. "All right. Yes. Give me that packet."

Having taken the money, she described what the pilot had been able to reveal to her after she had lowered his guard for him. (An oddly sweet pair of nights; but best not think about that.) "He doesn't know the coordinates yet, you realize," she finished. "Not even what kind of sun it is, except for the metals. It must be somewhere not too far off his assigned route. But he says that leaves thousands of possibilities."

"Or more." Rax forgot to control intonation. Was the sawing rhythm that came out of the speaker an equivalent of its equivalent of an awed whisper? "So many, many stars . . . a hundred billion in this one lost lonely dustmote of a galaxy . . . and we on the edge, remote in a spiral arm where they thin toward emptiness . . . what do we know, what can we master?"

The voice became flat and businesslike again. "This could be a prize worth contending for. We would pay well

24

for a report from you. Under certain circumstances, a million."

What Nicky said he was getting! And Leon's paying me a bare hundred thousand—Djana shook her head. "I'll be watched for quite a while, Rax, if Wayland turns out to be any use. What good is a fortune after you've been blasted?" She shivered. "Or they might be angry enough to brain-channel me and—" The cigarette scorched her fingers. She ground it into a disposer and reached for a new one. *A million credits,* she thought wildly. *A million packs of smokes. But no, that's not it. What you do is bank it and live off the interest. No huge income, but you'd be comfortable on it, and safe, and free, free—*

"You would require disappearance, certainly," Rax said. "That is part of the plan."

"Do you mean we . . . our boat. . . . would never come back?"

"Correct. The Navy will mount a search, with no result. Ammon will not soon be able to obtain another scout, and in the interim he can be diverted from his purpose or done away with. You can be taken to a suitably distant point, to Terra itself if you wish."

Djana started her cigarette. The taste was wrong. "What about, well, him?"

"Junior Lieutenant Flandry? No great harm need come if the matter is handled efficiently. For the sums involved, one can afford to hire technicians and equipment able to remove recent memories from him without damage to the rest of his personality. He can be left where he will soon be found. The natural assumption will be that he was captured by Merseians and hypnoprobed in a random-pattern search for information."

Rax hunched forward. "Let me make the proposition quite specific," it continued. "If Wayland turns out to be worthless, you simply report to Ammon as ordered. When it is safe, you seek me and tell me the details. I want especially to know as much about Flandry as you can extract from him. For example, has he anything more in mind concerning this mission than earning his bribe? You see, my organization may well have uses of its own for a buyable Navy officer. Since this puts you to no special effort or hazard, your compensation will be one hundred thousand credits."

Plus what I've already got in my purse, she exulted, *plus Leon's payment!*

"And if the moon is valuable?" she murmured.

"Then you must capture the boat. That should not be

25

difficult. Flandry will be unsuspicious. Furthermore, our agents will have seen to it that the crates supposed to contain impellers do not. That presents no problem; the storage cave is unguarded."

Djana frowned. "Huh? What for? How can he check out the place if he can't flit around in his spacesuit?"

"It will not be considered your fault if his judgment proves erroneous, for this or any other cause. But he should be able to do well enough; it is not as if this were a xenological expedition or the like. The reason for thus restricting his mobility is that he—young and reckless—will thereby be less likely to undertake things which could expose you, our contact, to danger."

"Welll!" Djana chuckled. "Nice of you."

"After Flandry is your prisoner, you will steer the boat through a volume whose coordinates will be given you," Rax finished. "This will bring you within detection range of a ship belonging to us, which will make rendezvous and take you aboard. Your reward will go to a million credits."

"Um-m-m . . ." *Check every angle, girl. The one you don't check is sure to be the one with a steel trap in it.* Djana flinched, recalling when certain jaws had punished her for disobedience to an influential person. Rallying, she asked: "Why not just trail the scout?"

"The space vibrations created by an operating hyperdrive are detectable, instantaneously, to a distance of about one light-year," Rax said, patient with her ignorance of technology. "That is what limits communications over any greater reach to physical objects such as letters or couriers. If our vessel can detect where Flandry's is, his can do likewise and he may be expected to take countermeasures."

"I see." Djana sat a while longer, thinking her way forward. At last she looked up and said: "By Jesus, you do tempt me. But I'll be honest, I'm scared. I know damn well I'm being watched, ever since I agreed to do this job, and Leon might take it into his head to give me a narcoquiz. You know?"

"This has also been provided for." Rax pointed. "Behind yonder door is a hypnoprobe with amnesiagenic attachments. I am expert in its use. If you agree to help us for the compensation mentioned, you will be shown the rendezvous coordinates and memorize them. Thereafter your recollection of this night will be driven from your consciousness."

"What?" It was as if a hand closed around Djana's

26

heart. She sagged back into her chair. The cigarette dropped from cold fingers.

"Have no fears," the goblin said. "Do not confuse this with zombie-making. There will be no implanted compulsions, unless you count a posthypnotic suggestion making you want to explore Flandry's mind and persuade him to show you how to operate the boat. You will simply awaken tomorrow in a somewhat disorganized state, which will soon pass except that you cannot remember what happened after you arrived here. The suggestion will indicate a night involving drugs, and the money in your purse will indicate the night was not wasted. I doubt you will worry long about the matter, especially since you are soon heading into space."

"I—well—I don't touch the heavy drugs, Rax—"

"Perhaps your client spiked a drink. To continue: Your latent memories will be buried past the reach of any mere narcoquiz. Two alternative situations will restimulate them. One will be an interview where Flandry has told Ammon Wayland is worthless. The other will be his telling you, on the scene, that it is valuable. In either case, full knowledge will return to your awareness and you can take appropriate action."

Djana shook her head. "I've seen . . . brain-channeled . . . brain-burned—no," she choked. Every detail in the room, a checkerboard pattern on a lounger, a moving wrinkle on Rax's face, the panels of the inner door, stood before her with nightmare sharpness. "No. I won't."

"I do not speak of slave conditioning," the other said. "That would make you too inflexible. Besides, it takes longer than the hour or so we dare spend. I speak of a voluntary bargain with us which includes your submitting to a harmless cue-recall amnesia."

Djana rose. The knees shook beneath her. "You, you, you could make a mistake. No. I'm going. Let me out." She reached into her purse.

She was too late. The slugthrower had appeared. She stared down its muzzle. "If you do not cooperate tonight," Rax told her, "you are dead. Therefore, why not give yourself a chance to win a million credits? They can buy you liberation from what you are."

CHAPTER

IV

The next stage of the adventure came a month afterward. That was when the mortal danger began.

The sun that men had once named Mimir burned with four times the brightness of Sol; but at a distance of five astronomical units it showed tiny, a bluish-white firespot too intense for the unshielded eye. Covering its disc with a finger, you became able to see the haze around it—gas, dust, meteoroids, a nebula miniature in extent but thick as any to be found anywhere in the known universe—and the spearpoints of light created by reflection within that nebula. Elsewhere, darkness swarmed with remoter stars and the Milky Way foamed around heaven.

Somewhat more than four million kilometers from the scoutboat, Regin spread over two and a half times the sky diameter of Luna seen from Terra. The day side of the giant planet cast sunlight blindingly off clouds in its intensely compressed atmosphere. The night side had an ashen-hued glow of its own, partly from aurora, partly from luminosity rebounding off a score of moons.

They included Wayland. Though no bigger than Luna, the satellite dominated the forward viewscreen: for the boat was heading straight down out of orbit. The vision of stark peaks, glacier fields, barren plains, craters old and eroded or new and raw, was hardly softened by a thin blanket of air.

Flandry sent his hands dancing over the pilot board. Technically Comet class, his vessel was antiquated and minimally equipped. Without a proper conning computer, he must make his approach manually. It didn't bother him. Having gotten the needful data during free fall around the globe, he had only to keep observant of his instruments and direct the grav drive accordingly. For him it was a dance with the boat for partner, to the lilt of cosmic forces; and indeed he whistled a waltz tune through his teeth.

Nonetheless he was taut. The faint vibrations of power, rustle and chemical-sharp odor of ventilation, pull of the

28

interior weightmaking field, stood uncommonly strong in his awareness. He heard the blood beat in his ears.

Harnessed beside him, Djana exclaimed: "You're not aiming for the centrum. You're way off."

He spared her a look. Even now he enjoyed the sight. "Of course," he said.

"What? Why?"

"Isn't it obvious? Something mighty damn strange is going on there. I'm not about to bull in. Far better we weasel in." He laughed. "Though I'd rather continue tom-catting."

Her features hardened. "If you try to pull any—"

"Ah-ah. No bitching." Flandry gave his attention back to the board and screens. His voice went on, abstractedly: "I'm surprised at you. I am for a fact. A hooker so tough albeit delectable, not taking for granted we'd reconnoiter first. I'm going to land us in that crater—see it? Ought to be firm ground, though we'll give it a beam test before we cut the engine. With luck, any of those flying weirdies we saw that happens to pass overhead should register us as another piece of meteorite. Not that I expect any will chance by. This may be a miniworld, but it wears a lot of real estate. I'll leave you inboard and take a ver-ree cautious lookabout. If all goes well, we'll do some encores, working our way closer. And don't think I don't wish a particularly sticky hell be constructed for whatever coprolite brain it was that succeeded in packing the impeller cases with oxygen bottles."

He had not made that discovery until he was nearing Regin and had broken out the planetside gear Ammon had assembled to his order. You didn't need personal flying units on routine surveillance. The last thing you were supposed to do was land anywhere. They weren't even included in your emergency equipment. If you ran into trouble, they couldn't help you.

I should have checked the whole lot when we loaded it aboard on Planet Eight, he thought. *I'm guilty of taking something for granted. How Max Abrams would ream me out!* . . . *Well, I guess Intelligence agents learn their trade through sad experience like everybody else.*

After a string of remarks that made Djana herself blush, he had seriously considered aborting the Wayland mission. But no. Too many hazards were involved in a second try, starting with the difficulty of convincing his fellows that breakdowns had delayed him twice in a row. And what harm could an utterly lifeless ball of rock do him?

Strangely, the enigmatic things he had seen from orbit increased his determination to go down. Or perhaps that wasn't so strange. He was starved for action. Besides, at his age he dared not admit to any girl that he could be scared.

His whetted senses perceived that she shivered. It was for the first time in their voyage. But then, she was a creature of cities and machinery, not of the Big Deep.

And it was a mystery toward which they descended: where a complex of robots ought to have been at work, or at least passively waiting out the centuries, an inexplicable crisscross of lines drawn over a hundred square kilometers in front of the old buildings, and a traffic of objects like nothing ever seen before except in bad dreams. Daunting, yes. On a legitimate errand, Flandry would have gone back for reinforcements. But that was impractical under present circumstances.

Briefly, he felt a touch of pity for Djana. He knew she was as gentle, loving, and compassionate as a cryogenic drill. But she was beautiful (small, fine-boned, exquisite features, great blue eyes, honey-gold hair), which he considered a moral virtue. Apart from insisting that he prepare meals—and he was undoubtedly far the superior cook—she had accepted the cramped austerity of the boat with wry good humor. During their three weeks of travel she had given him freely of her talents, which commanded top price at home. While her formal education in other fields was scanty, between bouts she had proved an entertaining talkmate. Half enemy she might be, but Flandry had allowed himself the imprudent luxury of falling slightly in love with her, and felt he was a little in her debt. No other scouting sweep had been as pleasant!

Now she faced the spacefarer's truth, that the one thing we know for certain about this universe is that it is implacable. He wanted to reach across and console her.

But the vessel was entering atmosphere. A howl began to penetrate the hull, which bucked.

"Come on, *Jake*," Flandry said. "Be a good girl."

"Why do you always call the boat *Jake*?" his companion asked, obviously trying to get her mind off the crags lancing toward her.

"*Giacobini-Zinner* is ridiculous," he answered, "and the code letters can't be fitted into anything bawdy." *I refrain from inquiring what you were called as a child*, he thought. *I prefer not to believe in, say, an Ermintrude Bugglethwaite who invested in a, ah, house name and a to-*

30

tal-body biosculp job. . . . . "Quiet, please. This is tricky work. Thin air means high-velocity winds."

The engine growled. Interior counteracceleration force did not altogether compensate for lurching; the deck seemed to stagger. Flandry's hands flew, his feet shoved pedals, occasionally he spoke an order to the idiot-grade central computer that the boat did possess. But he'd done this sort of thing before, often under more difficult conditions. He'd make planetfall without real trouble—

The flyers came.

He had scarcely a minute's warning of them. Djana screamed as they whipped from a veil of driving gray cloud. They were metal, bright in the light of Mimir and of Regin's horizon-scraping dayside crescent. Wide, ribbed wings upbore sticklike torsos, grotesque empennage, beaks and claws. They were much smaller than the spacecraft, but they numbered a score or worse.

They attacked. They could do no real harm directly. Their hammering and scraping resounded wild in the hull. But however frail by the standards of a real ship, a Comet was built to resist heavier buffetings.

They did, though, rock it. Wheeling and soaring, they darkened vision. More terribly, they interfered with radar, sonic beams, every probing of every instrument. Suddenly, except for glimpses when they flashed aside, Flandry was piloting blind. The wind sent his craft reeling.

He stabbed forth flame out of the single spitgun in the nose. A flyer exploded in smoke and fragments. Another, wing sheared across, spun downward to destruction. The rest were too many, too quickly reacting. "We've got to get out of here!" he heard himself yell, and crammed on power.

Shock smashed through him. Metal shrieked. The world whirled in the screens. For an instant, he saw what had happened. Without sight or sensors, in the turbulence of the air, he had descended further than he knew. His spurt of acceleration was not vertical. It had sideswiped a mountaintop.

No time for fear. He became the boat. Two thrust cones remained, not enough to escape with but maybe enough to set down on and not spatter. He ignored the flock and fought for control of the drunkenly unbalanced grav drive. If he made a straight tail-first backdown, the force would fend off the opposition; he'd have an uncluttered scan aft, which he could project onto one of the pilot board screens and use for an eyeballed landing. That was *if* he could hold her upright.

If not, well, it had been fun living.

The noise lessened to wind-whistle, engine stutter, drumbeat of beaks. Through it he was faintly astonished to hear Djana. He shot her a glance. Her eyes were closed, her hands laid palm to palm, and from her lips poured ancient words, over and over. "Hail Mary, full of grace—"

Her? And he'd thought he'd gotten to know her!

CHAPTER

V

They landed skull-rattlingly hard. Weakened members in the boat gave way with screeches and thumps. But they landed.

At once Flandry bent himself entirely to the spitgun. Locked onto target after target, the beam flashed blue among the attackers that wheeled overhead. A winged thing slanted downward and struck behind the rim of the crater where he had settled. A couple of others took severe damage and limped off. The remainder escorted them. In a few minutes the last was gone from sight.

No—wait—high above, out of range, a hovering spark in murky heaven? Flandry focused a viewscreen and turned up the magnification. "Uh-huh," he nodded. "One of our playmates has stayed behind to keep a beady eye on us."

"O-o-o-oh-h-h," Djana whimpered.

"Pull yourself together," he snapped. "You know how. Insert Part A in Slot B, bolt to Section C, et cetera. In case nobody's told you, we have a problem."

Mainly he was concerned with studying the indicators on the board while he unharnessed. Some air had been lost, and replenished from the reserve tanks, but there was no further leakage. Evidently the hull had cracked, not too badly for self-sealing but enough to make him doubt the feasibility of returning to space without repairs. Inboard damage must be worse, for the grav field was off—he moved under Wayland's half a terrestrial *g* with a bounding ease that roused no enthusiasm in him—and, oh-oh indeed, the nuclear generator was dead. Light, heat, air and water cycles, everything was running off the accumulators.

"Keep watch," he told Djana. "If you see anything peculiar, feel free to holler."

He went aft, past the chaos of galley and head, the more solidly battened-down instrument and life-support centers, to the engine room. An hour's inspection confirmed neither his rosiest hopes nor his sharpest fears. It was possible to fix *Jake,* and probably wouldn't take long: if and only if shipyard facilities were brought to bear.

33

"So what else is new?" he said and returned forward.

Djana had been busy. She stood in the conn with all the small arms aboard on a seat behind her—the issue blaster and needler, his private Merseian war knife—except for the stun pistol she had brought herself. That was holstered on her flank. She rested a hand on its iridivory butt.

"What the deuce?" Flandry exclaimed. "I might even ask, What the trey?"

He started toward her. She drew the gun. "Halt," she said. Her soprano had gone flat.

He obeyed. She could drop him as he attacked, in this space where there was no room to dodge, and secure him before he regained consciousness. Of course, he could perhaps work free of any knots she was able to tie, but— He swallowed his dismay and studied her. The panic was gone, unless it dwelt behind that whitened skin and drew those lips into disfiguring straight lines.

"What's wrong?" he asked slowly. "My intentions are no more shocking than usual."

"Maybe nothing's wrong, Nicky." She attempted a smile. "I've got to be careful. You understand that, don't you? You're an Imperial officer and I'm riding Leon Ammon's rocket. Maybe we can keep on working together. And maybe not. What's happened here?"

He collected his wits. "Int'resting question," he said. "If you think this is a trap for you—well, really, my sweet, you know quite well no functional trap is that elaborate. I'm every bit as baffled as you . . . and worried, if that's any consolation. I want nothing at the moment but to get back with hide entire to vintage wine, gourmet food, good conversation, good music, good books, good tobacco, a variety of charming ladies, and everything else that civilization is about."

He was ninety-nine percent honest. The remaining one percent involved pocketing the rest of his million. Though not exclusively . . .

The girl didn't relax. "Well, can we?"

He told her what the condition of the boat was.

She nodded. Wings of amber-colored hair moved softly past delicate high cheekbones. "I thought that was more or less it," she said. "What do you figure to do?"

Flandry shifted stance and scratched the back of his neck. "Another interesting question. We can't survive indefinitely, you realize. Considering the outside temperature and other factors, I'd say that if we throttle all systems down to a minimum—and if we don't have to fire the spitgun again—we have accumulator energy for three months.

Food for longer, yes. But when the thermometer drops to minus a hundred, even steak sandwiches can only alleviate; they cannot cure."

She stamped a foot. "Will you stop trying to be funny!"

Why, I thought I was succeeding, Flandry wanted to say, *and incidentally, that motion of yours had fascinating effects in these snug-fitting pullovers we're wearing. Do it again?*

Djana overcame her anger. "We need help," she said.

"No point in trying to radio for it," Flandry said. "Air this thin supports too little ionosphere to send waves far past the horizon. Especially when the sun, however bright, is so distant. We might be able to bounce signals off Regin or another moon, except that that'd require aiming and monitoring gear *Jake* doesn't carry."

She stared at him in frank surprise. "Radio?"

"To the main computer at the mining centrum. It was originally a top-level machine, you know, complete with awareness—whatever it may have suffered since. And it commanded repair and maintenance equipment as well. If we could raise it and get a positive response, we should have the appropriate robots here in a few hours, and be off on the rest of my circuit in a few days."

Flandry smiled lopsidedly. "I wish now I had given it a call from orbit," he went on. "But with the skewball things we saw—we've lost that option. We shall simply have to march there in person and see what can be done."

Djana tensed anew. "I thought that's what you'd figure on," she said, winter bleak. "Nothing doing, lover. Too chancy."

"What else—"

She had hardly begun to reply when he knew. The heart stumbled in him.

"I didn't join you blind," she said. "I studied the situation first, whatever I could learn, including the standard apparatus on these boats. They carry several couriers each. One of those can make it back to Irumclaw in a couple of weeks, with a message telling where we are and what we're sitting on."

"But," he protested. "But. Listen, the assault on us wasn't likely the last attempt. I wouldn't guarantee we can hold out. We'd better leave here, duck into the hills—"

"Maybe. We'll play that as it falls. However, I am not passing up the main chance for survival, which is to bring in a Navy ship."

Djana's laugh was a yelp. "I can tell what you're thinking," she continued. "There I'll be, along on your job.

35

How many laws does that break? The authorities will check further. When they learn about your taking a bribe to do Ammon's work for him in an official vessel—I suppose at a minimum the sentence'll be life enslavement."

"What about you?" he countered.

Her lids drooped. Her lips closed and curved. She moved her hips from side to side. "Me? I'm a victim of circumstances. I was afraid to object, with you wicked men coercing me . . . till I got this chance to do the right thing. I'm sure I can make your commandant see it that way and give me an executive pardon. Maybe even a reward. We're good friends, really, Admiral Julius and me."

"You won't get through the wait here without my help," Flandry said. "Certainly not if we're attacked."

"I might or might not," she replied. Her expression thawed. "Nicky, darling, why must we fight? We'll have time to work out a plan for you. A story or—or maybe you can hide somewhere with supplies, and I can come back later and get you, I swear I will—" She swayed in his direction. "I swear I want to. You've been wonderful. I won't let you go."

"Regardless," he said, "you insist on sending a message."

"Yes."

"Can you launch a courier? What if I refuse?"

"Then I'll stun you, and tie you, and torture you till you agree," she said, turned altogether impersonal. "I know a lot about that."

Abruptly it blazed from her: "You'll never imagine how much I know! You'd die before I finished. Remember your boasting to me about the hardships you've met, a poor boy trying to get ahead in the service on nothing but ability? If you could've heard me laughing inside while I kissed you! *I* came up from slavery—in the Black Hole of Jihannath—what I've been through makes the worst they've thought of in Irumclaw Old Town look like a crèche game—I'm not going back to hell again—as God is my witness, I'm not!"

She drew a shaking breath and clamped the vizor once more into place. From a pocket she fetched a slip of paper. "This is the message," she said.

Flandry balanced on the balls of his feet. He might be able to take her, if he acted fast and luck fell his way . . . he just might. . . .

And swiftly as a stab, he knew the risk was needless. He gasped.

"What's the matter?" Djana's question wavered near hysteria.

He shook himself. "Nothing," he said. "All right, you win, let's ship your dispatch off."

The couriers were near the main airlock. He walked in advance, before her steady gun muzzle, though she knew the location. For that matter, the odds were she could figure out how to activate them herself. She had been quick to learn the method of putting the boat on a home-ward course—feed the destination coordinates to the auto-pilot, lock the manual controls, et cetera—when he met her request for precautionary instruction. These gadgets, four in number, were simpler yet.

Inside each torpedo shape—120 centimeters long, but light enough for a man to lift under Terran gravity—were packed the absolute minimum of hyperdrive and grav-drive machinery; sensors and navigational computer to guide it toward a preset goal; radio to beep when it neared; accumulators for power; and a tiny space for the payload, which could be a document, a tape, or whatever else would fit.

Ostentatiously obedient, Flandry opened one compart-ment and stepped aside while Djana laid in her letter and closed the shell. Irumclaw's coordinates were stenciled on it for easy reference and she watched him turn the control knobs. He slid the courier forward on the launch rack. Pausing, he said: "I'd like to program this for a sixty-sec-ond delay, if you don't mind."

"Why?"

"So we can get back to the conn and watch it take off. To be sure it does, you know."

"M-m-m—that makes sense." Djana hefted the gun. "I'm keeping you covered till it's outbound, understand."

"Logical. Afterward, can we both be uncovered?"

"Be still!"

Flandry started the mechanism and returned forward with her. They stared out.

The view was of desolation. *Jake* lay close by the crater wall, which sloped steeply aloft until its rim stood fanged in heaven, three kilometers above. Its palisades reached so far that they vanished under the near horizon before their opposite side became visible. The darkling rock was streaked with white, that also covered the floor: carbon dioxide and ammonia snow. This was beginning to vapor-ize in Wayland's sixteen-day time of sunlight; fogs boiled and mists steamed, exposing the bluish gleam of eternal water ice.

Overhead the sky was deep violet, almost black. Stars glittered wanly across most of it, for at this early hour Mimir's fierce disc barely cleared the ringwall in that area where the latter went behind the curve of the world. Regin was half a dimness mottled with intricate cloud patterns, half a shining like burnished steel.

A whitter of wind came in through the hull.

Behind Flandry, Djana said with unexpected wistfulness: "When the courier's gone, Nicky, will you hold me? Will you be good to me?"

He made no immediate reply. His shoulder and stomach muscles ached from tension.

The torpedo left its tube. For a moment it hovered, while the idiot pseudo-brain within recognized it was on a solid body and which way was up. It rose. Once above atmosphere, it would take sights on beacons such as Betelgeuse and lay a course to Irumclaw.

Except—yes! Djana wailed. Flandry whooped.

The spark high above had struck. As one point of glitter, the joined machines staggered across the sky.

Flandry went to the viewscreen and set the magnification. The torpedo had nothing but a parchment-thin aluminum skin, soon ripped by the flyer's beak while the flyer's talons held tight. The courier had ample power to shake off its assailant, but not the acumen to do so. Besides, the stresses would have wrecked it anyway. It continued to rise, but didn't get far before some critical circuit was broken. That killed it. The claws let go and it plummeted to destruction.

"I *thought* that'd happen," Flandry murmured.

The flyer resumed its station. Presently three others joined it. "They must've sensed our messenger, or been called," Flandry said. "No use trying to loft more, eh? We need their energy packs worse for other things."

Djana, who had stood numbed, cast her gun aside and crumpled weeping into his arms. He stroked her hair and made soothing noises.

At last she pulled herself together, looked at him, and said, still gulping and hiccoughing: "You're glad, aren't you?"

"Well, I can't say I'm sorry," he admitted.

"Y-y-you'd rather be dead than—"

"Than a slave? Yes, cliché or not, 'fraid so."

She considered him for a while that grew. "All right," she said most quietly. "That makes two of us."

CHAPTER

VI

He had topped the ringwall when the bugs found him.

His aim was to inspect the flyer which had crashed on the outer slope, while Djana packed supplies for the march. Perhaps he could get some clue as to what had gone wrong here. The possibility that those patrolling would spot him and attack seemed among the least of the hazards ahead. He could probably find a cave or crag or crevasse in time, a shelter where they couldn't get at him, on the rugged craterside. Judiciously applied at short range, the blaster in his hip sheath ought to rid him of them, in view of what the spitgun had accomplished—unless, of course, they summoned so many reinforcements that he ran out of charge.

Nothing happened. Tuning his spacesuit radio through its entire range of reception, he came upon a band where there was modulation: clicks and silences, a code reeling off with such speed that in his ears it sounded almost like an endless ululation, high-pitched and unhuman. He was tempted to transmit a few remarks on those frequencies, but decided not to draw unnecessary attention to himself. At their altitude, he might well be invisible to the flyers.

The rest of the available radio spectrum was silent, except for the seethe and crackle of cosmic static. And the world was silent, except for the moan of wind around him, the crunching of snow and rattling of stones as his boots struck, the noise of his own breath and heartbeat. The crater floor was rock, ice, drift of snow and mists, wan illumination that would nonetheless have burned him with ultraviolet rays had his faceplate let them past. Clouds drove ragged across alien constellations and the turbulent face of Regin. The crater wall lifted brutal before him.

Climbing it was not too difficult. Erosion had provided ample footing and handholds; and in this gravity, even burdened with space armor he was lighter than when nude under Terran pull. He adapted to the changed ratio of weight and inertia with an ease that would have been unconscious had he not remembered it was going to cause Djana some trouble and thereby slow the two of them down. Other than keeping a nervous eye swiveling skyward, the chief nuisance he suffered was due to imperfections of the air renewal and thermostatic units. He was soon hot, sweating, and engulfed in stench.

I'll be sure to fix that before we start! he thought. *And give the service crew billy hell when (if) I return.* Momentarily, the spirit sagged in him: *What's the use? They're sloppy because the higher echelons are incompetent because the Empire no longer really cares about holding this part of the marches. . . . In my grandfather's day we were still keeping what was ours, mostly. In my father's day, the slogan became "conciliation and consolidation," which means retreat. Is my day—my very own personal bit of daylight between the two infinite darknesses—is it going to turn into the Long Night?*

He clamped his teeth together and climbed more vigorously. *Not if I can help it!*

The bugs appeared.

They hopped from behind boulders and ice banks, twenty or more, soaring toward him. Some thirty centimeters long, they had ten claw-footed legs each, a tail ending in twin spikes, a head on which half a dozen antennae moved. Mimir's light shimmered purple off their intricately armored bodies.

For a second Flandry seriously wondered if he had lost his mind. The old records said Wayland was barren, always had been, always would be. He had expected nothing else. Life simply did not evolve where cold was this deep and permanent, air this tenuous, metal this dominant, background radiation this high. And supposing a strange version of it could, Mimir was a young star, that had coalesced with its planets only a few hundred megayears ago from a nebula enriched in heavy atoms by earlier stellar generations; the system hadn't yet finished condensing, as witness the haze around the sun and the rate of giant meteorite impacts; there had not been time for life to start.

Thus Flandry's thought flashed. It ended when the shapes were murderously upon him.

Two landed on his helmet. He heard the clicks, felt the astonishing impact. Looking down, he saw others at his waist, clinging to his legs, swarming around his boots. Jaws champed, claws dug. They found the joints in his armor and went to work.

No living thing smaller than a Llynathawrian elephant wolf should have been able to make an impression on the alloys and plastics that encased Flandry. He saw shavings

40

peel off and fall like sparks of glitter. He saw water vapor puff white from the first pinhole by his left ankle. The creature that made it gnawed industriously on.

Flandry yelled an obscenity. He shook one loose and manged to kick it. The shock of striking that mass hurt his toes. The bug didn't arc far, nor was it injured. It sprang back to the fray. Flandry was trying to pluck another off. It clung too strongly for him.

He drew his blaster, set it to needle beam and low intensity, laid the muzzle against the carapace, and pulled the trigger.

The creature did not smoke or explode or do whatever else a normal organism would. But after two or three seconds it let go, dropped to the ground and lay inert.

The rest continued their senseless, furious attack. Flandry cooked them off him and slew those that hadn't reached him with a series of energy bolts. No organism that size, that powerful, that heavily shelled, ought to have been that vulnerable to his brief, frugal beams.

The last two were on his back where he couldn't see them. He widened the blaster muzzle and fanned across the air renewal unit. They dropped off him. The heat skyrocketed the temperature in his suit and drove gas faster out of the several leaks. Flandry's eardrums popped painfully. His head roared and whirled.

Training paid off. Scarcely aware of what he did, he slapped sealpatches on the holes and bled the reserve tank for a fresh atmosphere. Only then did he sit down, gasp, shudder, and finally wet his mummy-dry mouth from the water tube.

Afterward he was able to examine the dead bugs. Throwing a couple of them into his pack, he resumed climbing. From the top of the ringwall he discerned the wrecked flyer and slanted across talus and ice patches to reach it. The crash had pretty well fractured it to bits, which facilitated study. He collected a few specimen parts and returned to *Jake*.

The trip was made in a growingly grim silence, which he scarcely broke when he re-entered the boat. Aloneness and not knowing had ground Djana down. She sped to welcome him. He gave her a perfunctory kiss, demanded food and a large pot of coffee, and brushed past her on his way to the workshop.

41

CHAPTER
VII

They had about 200 kilometers to go. That was the distance, according to the maps Flandry had made in orbit, from the scoutboat's resting place to a peak so high that a transmission from it would be line-of-sight with some of the towering radio transceiver masts he had observed at varying separations from the old computer centrum.

"We don't want to get closer than we must," he explained to the girl. "We want plenty of room for running, if we find out that operations have been taken over by something that eats people."

She swallowed. "Where could we run to?"

"That's a good question. But I won't lie down and die gracefully. I'm far too cowardly for that."

She didn't respond to his smile. He hoped she hadn't taken his remark literally, even though it contained a fair amount of truth.

The trip could be shortened by crossing two intervening maria. Flandry refused. "I prefer to skulk," he said, laying out a circuitous path through foothills and a mountain range that offered hiding places. While it would often make the going tough, and Djana was inexperienced and not in training, and they would be burdened with Ammon's supplies and planetside gear, he hoped they could average thirty or forty kilometers per twenty-four hours. A pitiful few factors worked in their favor. There was the mild gravity and the absence of rivers to ford and brush to struggle through. There was the probably steady weather. Since Wayland always turned the same face to Regin, there was continuous daylight for the span of their journey, except at high noon when the planet would eclipse Mimir. There was an ample supply of stimulants. *And,* Flandry reflected, *it helps to travel scared.*

He decreed a final decent meal before departure, and music and lovemaking and a good sleep while the boat's sensors kept watch. The party fell rather flat; Djana was too conscious that this might be the last time. Flandry made no reproaches. He did dismiss any vague ideas he might

42

have entertained about trying for a long-term liaison with her.

They loaded up and marched. More accurately, they scrambled, across the crater wall and into a stretch of sharp hills and wind-polished slippery glaciers. Flandry allowed ten minutes' rest per hour. He spent most of those periods with map, gyrocompass, and sextant, making sure they were still headed right. When Djana declared she could do no more, he said calculatedly, "Yes, I understand; you're no use off your back." She spat her rage and jumped to her feet.

I mustn't drive her too hard, Flandry realized. *Gradual strengthening will get us where we're going faster. In fact, without that she might not make it at all.*

Does that matter?

Yes, it does. I can't abandon her.

Why not? She'd do the same for me.

Um-m-m . . . I don't know exactly why . . . let's say that in spite of everything, she's a woman. Waste not, want not.

When she did begin reeling as she walked, he agreed to pitch camp and did most of the chores alone.

First he selected a spot beneath an overhanging cliff. "So our winged chums won't see us," he explained chattily, "or drop on us their equivalent of what winged chums usually drop. You will note, however, that an easy route will take us onto the top of the cliff, if we should have groundborne callers. From there we can shoot, throw rocks, and otherwise hint to them that they're not especially welcome." Slumped in exhaustion against a boulder, she paid him no heed.

He inflated the insulating floor of the sealtent and erected its framework. The wind gave him trouble, flapping the fabric he stretched across until he got it secured. Because the temperature had risen to about minus fifty, he didn't bother with extra layers, but merely filled the cells of the one skin with air.

To save accumulator charge, he worked the pump by hand, and likewise when it evacuated the tent's interior. Extreme decompression wasn't needed, since the Waylander atmosphere was mostly noble gases and nitrogen. The portable air renewer he had placed inside, together with a glower for heat, took care of remaining poisonous vapors and excess carbon dioxide, once he had refilled the tent with oxygen at 200 millibars. (The equipment for all this was heavy. But it was indispensable, at least until Djana got into such condition that she didn't frequently need the relief of shirtsleeve environment. And she'd better! Given

43

the limitations of what they could carry, they could make possibly fifteen stops that utilized it.) While renewer and glower did their work, Flandry chipped water ice to melt for drinking and cooking.

They entered through the plastic airlock. He showed Djana how to bleed her spacesuit down to ambient pressure. When they had taken off their armor, she lay on the floor and watched him with eyes glazed by fatigue. He fitted together his still, put it on the glower, and filled it with ice. "Why are you doing that?" she whispered.

"Might have unpleasant ingredients," he answered. "Gases like ammonia come off first and are taken up by the activated colloids in this bottle. We can't let them contaminate our air; our one renewer's busy handling the stuff we breathe out; and besides, when we strike camp I must pump as big a fraction as I can manage back into its tank. When the water starts boiling, I shut the valve to the gas-impurity flask and open the one to the water can. We can't risk heavy metal salts, especially on a world where they must be plentiful. Doesn't take but a micro quantity of plutonium, say, this far from medical help, to kill you in quite a nasty fashion. A propos, I suppose you know we daren't smoke in a pure oxy atmosphere."

She shuddered and turned her glance from the desolation in the ports.

Dinner revived her somewhat. Afterward she sat hugging her legs, chin on knees, and watched him clean the utensils. In the cramped space, his movements were economical. "You were right," she said gravely. "I wouldn't have a prayer without you."

"A hot meal, albeit freeze-dried, does beat pushing a concentrate bar through your chowlock and calling it lunch, eh?"

"You know what I mean, Nicky. What can I do?"

"You can take your turn watching for monsters," he said immediately.

She winced. "Do you really think—"

"No. I don't think. Too few data thus far to make it worth the trouble. Unhappily, though, one datum is the presence of two or more kinds of critter whose manners are as deplorable as they are inexplicable."

"But they're machines!"

"Are they?"

She stared at him from under tangled tawny bangs. He said while he labored: "Where does 'robot' leave off and 'organism' begin? For hundreds of years there've been sensor-computer-effector systems more intricate and versatile than some kinds of organic life. They function, perceive,

44

ingest, have means to repair damage and to be reproduced; they homeostatize, if that horrible word is the one I want; certain of them think. None of it works identically with the systems evolved by organic animals and sophonts —but it works, and toward very similar ends.

"Those bugs that attacked me have metal exoskeletons underneath that purple enamel, and electronic insides. That's why they succumbed so easily to my blaster: high heat conductivity, raising the temperature of components designed for Wayland's natural conditions. But they're machinery as elaborate as any I've ever ruined. As I told you, I hadn't the time or means to do a proper job of dissection. As near as I could tell, though, they run off accumulators. Their feelers are magnificently precise sensors— magnetic, electric, radionic, thermal, et cetera. They have optical and audio systems as well. In fact, with one exception, they're such gorgeous engineering that it's a semantic quibble whether to call them robots or artificial animals.

"Same thing, essentially, for the flyers—which, by the way, I'm tempted to call snapdragonflies. They get their lift from the wings and a VTOL turbojet; they use beak and claws to rip rather than grind metal; but they have sensors and computers akin to the bugs'. And they seem able to act more independently, as you'd expect with a larger 'brain.'"

He put away the last dish, settled back, and longed for a cigarette. "What do you mean by 'one exception'?" Djana asked.

"I can imagine a robotic ecology, based on self-reproducing solar-cell units that'd perform the equivalent of photosynthesis," Flandry said. "I seem to recall it was actually experimented with once. But these things we've met don't have anything I can identify as being for nourishment, repair, or reproduction. No doubt they have someplace to go for replacement parts and energy recharges—someplace where new ones are also manufactured—most likely the centrum area. But what about the wrecked ones? There doesn't seem to be any interest in reclaiming those marvelous parts, or even the metal. It's not an ecology, then; it's open-ended. Those machines have no purpose except destruction."

He drew breath. "In spite of which," he said, "I don't believe they're meant for guarding this world or any such job. Because who save a lunatic would build a fighting robot and omit guns?

"Somehow, Djana, Wayland's come down with a plague of monsters. Until we know how many of what kinds, I

45

suggest we proceed on the assumption that everything we meet will want to do us in."

A few times in the course of the next several Terran days, the humans concealed themselves when shapes passed by. These might be flyers cruising far overhead, in one case stooping on some prey hidden by a ridge. Or a pair of dog-sized, huge-jawed, sensor-bristling hunters loped six-legged on a quest; or a bigger object, horned and spike-tailed, rumbled on caterpillar treads along the bottom of a ravine. Twice Flandry lay prone and watched combats: bugs swarming over a walking red globe with lobsterish claws; a constrictor shape entangled with a mobile battering ram. Both end results appeared to confirm his deductions. The vanquished were left where they fell while the victors resumed prowling. Remnants from earlier battles indicated the same aftermath.

Otherwise the journey was nothing but a struggle to make distance. There was little opportunity while afoot, little wakefulness while at rest, to think about the significance of what had been seen. Nor did Flandry worry about encountering a killer. If it happened, it happened. On the whole, he didn't expect that kind of trouble . . . yet. This was too vast and rugged a land for any likelihood of it. Given due caution, he and Djana ought to make their first objective. What occurred after that might be a different story.

He did notice that the radio traffic got steadily thicker on the nonstandard band the robots used. No surprise. He was nearing what had been the center of operations, which must still be the center of whatever the hell was going on nowadays.

Hell indeed, he thought through the dullness of the exhaustion. *Did somebody sabotage Wayland, maybe long ago, by installing a predator factory? Or was it perhaps an accident? People may have fought hereabouts, and I suppose a nearby explosion could derange the main computer?*

None of the guesses seemed reasonable. The beast machines couldn't offer effective opposition to modern weapons. They threatened the lives of two marooned humans; but a single spacecraft, well-armed, well-equipped with detectors, crew alerted to the situation, could probably annihilate them with small difficulty. That fact ruled out sabotage—didn't it? As for damage to the ultimate control engine: Imprimis, it must have had heavy shielding, plus extensive self-repair capability, the more so in view of the meteorite hazard. Secundus, assuming it did sustain per-

46

manent harm, that implied a loss of components; it would then scarcely be able to design and produce these superbly crafted gargoyles.

Flandry gave up wondering.

The time came when he and Djana halted within an hour of the mountaintop that was their goal. They found a cave, screened by tall pinnacles, wherein they erected the sealtent. "It's not going any further," the man said. "Among other reasons, you know how long it takes to raise and to knock down again; and we can't stand many more losses of unrecovered oxygen each time we break camp. So if we don't succeed in getting help, and in particular if we provoke a hunt for us, the burden won't be worth carrying. This is a nice, hard-to-find, defensible spot to sit in."

"When do we call?" the girl asked.

"When we've corked off for about twelve hours," Flandry said. "I want to be well rested."

She herself was tired enough that she dropped straight into sleep.

In the "morning" his spirits were somewhat restored. He whistled as he led the way upward, and when he stood on the peak he declaimed, "I name thee Mt. Maidens." All the while, though, his attention ranged ahead.

Behind and on either side was the familiar jumble of rock, ice, and inky shadows. Above gloomed the sky, its scattered stars and clouds, Mimir's searing brilliance now very near the dim, bright-edged shield of Regin. The wind whimpered around. He was glad to be inside his warm if smelly armor.

Ahead, as his topographical maps had revealed, the mountain dropped with a steepness that would have been impossible under higher gravity. The horizon was flat, betokening the edge of the plain where the centrum lay, and the squares he had seen, and he knew not what else. Through binoculars he made out the cruciform tops of four radio transceiver masts. Those had risen since man abandoned Wayland; others were scattered about in the wilds; from orbit, he had identified a few as being under construction by robots of recognizable worker form. He had considered making for one of those sites instead of here, but decided against it. That kind of robot was too specialized, also in its "brain," to understand his problem. Besides, the nearest was dangerously far from *Jake*'s resting place.

He unfolded a light tripod-based directional transmitter. He plugged in the ancillary apparatus, including a jack to his own helmet radio. Squatting, he directed the assembly

47

in its rotation until it had locked onto one of the masts. Djana waited. Her face showed still more gaunt and grimy than his, her eyes hollow and fever-bright.

"Here goes," Flandry said.

"O God, have mercy, help us," breathed in his earplugs. He wondered briefly, pityingly, if religion was what had kept her going, ever since her nightmare childhood. But he had to tell her to keep silence.

He called on the standard band. "Two humans, shipwrecked, in need of assistance. Respond." And again. And again. Nothing answered but the fire-crackle of cosmic energies.

He tried on the robots' band. The digital code chattered with no alteration that he could detect.

He tried other frequencies.

After an hour or more, he unplugged and rose. His muscles ached, his mouth was parched, his voice came hoarse out of a roughened throat. "No go, I'm afraid."

Djana had been seated on the sanitary unit from her pack, which doubled as a stool protecting against the elemental cold beneath. He had watched her shrink further and further into herself. "So we're finished," she mumbled.

He sighed. "The circumstances could be more promising. The big computer should've replied instantly to a distress call." He paused. The wind blew, the stars jeered. He straightened. "I'm going for a first-hand look."

"Out in the open?" She scrambled erect. Her gauntlets closed spastically around his. "You'll be swarmed and killed!"

"Not necessarily. We saw from the boat, things do appear to be different yonder from elsewhere. For instance, none of the accumulated wreckage you'd expect if fighting went on. Anyhow, it's our last resort." Flandry patted her in a fatherly way, which he might as well under present conditions. "You'll stay in the tent, of course, and wait for me."

She moistened her lips. "No, I'll come along," she said.

"Whoa! You could get scragged."

"Rather that than starve to death, which I will if you don't make it. I won't handicap you, Nicky. Not any more. If we aren't loaded down the way we were, I can keep up with you. And I'll be extra hands and eyes."

He pondered. "Well, if you insist." *She's more likely to be an asset than not—a survivor type like her.*

Sardonically: *Yes, just like her. I suspect she's got more than one motive for this. Exemplia gratia, to make damn sure I don't gain anything she doesn't get in on.*

Not that a profit seems plausible.

48

CHAPTER

VIII

As they neared the plain, Mimir went into eclipse.

The last arc of brilliance edging Regin vanished with the sun. Instead, the planet showed as a flattened black disc overlaid with faint, flickering auroral glow and ringed with sullen red where light was refracted through atmosphere.

Flandry had anticipated it. The stars, suddenly treading forth many and resplendent, and the small crescents of two companion moons, ought to give sufficient illumination for cautious travel. At need, he and Djana could use their flashbeams, though he would rather not risk drawing attention.

He had forgotten how temperature would tumble. Fog started forming within minutes, until the world was swirling shapeless murk. It gave way after a while to snow borne on a lashing, squealing wind. Carbon dioxide mostly, he guessed; maybe some ammonia. He leaned into the thrust, squinted at his gyrocompass, and slogged on.

Djana caught his arm. "Shouldn't we wait?" he barely heard through the noise.

He shook his head before he remembered that to her he had become a shadow. "No. A chance to make progress without being spotted."

"First luck we've had. Thanks, Jesus!"

Flandry refrained from observing that when the storm ended they might be irrevocably far into a hostile unknown. What had they to lose?

For a time, as they groped, he thought the audio pickups in his helmet registered a machine rumble. Did he actually feel the ground quiver beneath some great moving mass? He changed direction a trifle, without saying anything to the girl.

In this region, eclipse lasted close to two hours. The station would have been located on farside, escaping the darknesses altogether, except for the offsetting advantage of having Regin high in the night sky. When full, the planet must flood this hemisphere with soft radiance, an impossibly beautiful sight.

Though I doubt the robots ever gave a damn about scenery, Flandry thought, peering down to guide his boots past boulders and drifts. *Unless maybe the central computer . . . yes, I suppose. Imperial technology doesn't use many fully conscious machines—little need for them when we're no longer adventuring into new parts of the galaxy —so I, at any rate, know less about them than my ancestors did. Still, I can guess that a "brain" that powerful would necessarily develop interests outside its regular work. Its function—its desire, to get anthropomorphic— was to serve the human masters. But in between prospectings, constructions, visiting ships, when routine could only have occupied a minor part of its capacity, did it turn sensors onto the night sky and admire?*

Daylight began to filter through the snowfall. The wind died to a soughing. The ground flattened rapidly. Before precipitation had quite ended, fog was back, the newly frozen gases subliming under Mimir's rays and recondensing in air.

Flandry said, low and by sonic transmission: "Radio silence. Move quiet as you can." It was hardly a needful order. Earplugs were loud with digital code and there came a metallic rattle from ahead.

Once more Wayland took Flandry by surprise. He had expected the mists to lift slowly, as they'd done near dawn, giving him and Djana time to make out something of what was around them before they were likely to be noticed. His observations in orbit had indicated as much. For minutes the whiteness did veil them. Two meters away, wet ice and rock, tumbling rivulets, steaming puddles, faded into smoky nothing.

It broke apart. Through the rifts he saw the plain and the machines. The holes widened with tearing rapidity. The fog turned into cloudlets which puffed aloft and vanished.

Djana screamed.

Knowledge struck through Flandry: *Damn me for a witling! Why didn't I think? It takes a long while to heat things up again after half a month of night. But not after two hours. And evaporation goes fast at low pressures. What I saw from space, and assumed were lingering ground hazes, were clouds higher up, like those I see steaming away above us—*

That was at the back of his brain. Most of him saw what surrounded him. The blaster sprang into his hand.

50

Though the mountain was not far behind, soaring from a knife-edge boundary, he and Djana had passed by the nearest radio mast and were down on the plain. Like other Waylander maria, it was not perfectly level; it rolled, reared in scattered needles and minor craters, seamed itself with narrow cracks, was bestrewn with rocks and overlaid in places by ice banks. The travelers had entered the section that was marked into squares. More than a kilometer apart, the lines ran arrow straight, east and west, north and south, further than he could see before curvature shut off vision. He happened to be near one and could identify it as a wide streak of black granules driven permanently into the stone.

What he truly saw in that moment was the robots.

A hundred meters to his right went three of the six-legged lopers. Somewhat further off on his left rolled a horned and treaded giant. Still further ahead, but not too far to catch him, straggled half a dozen different monstrosities. Bugs by the score leaped and crawled across the ground. Flyers were slanting down the sky. He threw a look to rear and saw retreat cut off by a set of legs upbearing a circular saw.

Djana cast herself on her knees. Flandry crouched above, teeth skinned, and waited in the racket of his heart for the first assailant.

There was none.

The killers ignored them.

Nor did they pay attention to each other.

While not totally unexpected, the relief sent Flandry's mind whirling. When he had recovered, he saw that the machines were converging on a point. Nothing appeared above the horizon; their goal was too distant. He knew what it was, though—the central complex of buildings.

Djana began to laugh, wilder and wilder. Flandry didn't think they could afford hysteria. He hauled her to her feet. "Turn off that braying before I shake it out of you!" When words didn't work, he took her by her ankles, held her upside down, and made his threat good.

While she sobbed and gulped and wrestled her way back to control, he held her in a more gentle embrace and studied the robots across her shoulder. Most were in poor shape, holes torn in their skins, limbs missing. No wonder he'd heard them rattle and clank in the fog. Some looked unhurt aside from minor scratches and dents. Probably their accumulators were about drained.

In the end, he could explain to her: "I always figured those which survived the battles would get recharge and

51

repair in this area. Um-m-m . . . it can't well serve all Wayland . . . I daresay the critters never wander extremely far from it . . . and we did spot construction work, the setup's being steadily expanded, probably new centers are planned. . . . Anyhow, this place is trucial. Elsewhere, they're programed to attack anything that moves and isn't like their own particular breed. Here, they're perfect lambs. Or so goes my current guess."

"W-we're safe, then?"

"I wouldn't swear to that. What's caused this whole insanity? But I do think we can proceed."

"Where to?"

"The centrum, of course. Giving those fellows a respectful berth. They seem to be headed offside. I imagine their R & R stations lie some ways from the main computer's old location."

"Old?"

"We don't know if it exists any longer," Flandry reminded her.

Nonetheless he walked with ebullience. He was still alive. How marvelous that his arms swung, his heels smote ground, his lungs inhaled, his unwashed scalp itched! Regin had begun to wax, the thinnest of bows drawing back from Mimir's incandescent arrowpoint. Elsewhere glittered stars. Djana walked silent, exhausted by emotion. She'd recover, and when he got her back inside the sealtent . . .

He was actually whistling as they crossed the next line. A moment later he took her arm and pointed. "Look," he said.

A new kind of robot was approaching from within the square. It was about the size of a man. The skin gleamed golden. Iridescence was lovely over the great batlike wings that helped the springing of its two long hoofed and spurred legs. The body was a horizontal barrel, a balancing tail behind, a neck and head rearing in front. With its goggling optical and erect audio sensors, its muzzle that perhaps held the computer, its mane of erect antennae, that head looked eerily equine. From its forepart, swivelmounted, thrust a lance.

"We could almost call it a rockinghorsefly, couldn't we?" Flandry said. "As for the bread-and-butterfly—" His classical reference was lost on the girl.

She screamed afresh when the robot wheeled and came toward them in huge leaps. The lance was aimed to kill.

CHAPTER

IX

Djana was the target. She stood paralyzed. "Run!" Flandry bawled. He sped to intercept. The gun flamed in his grasp. Sparks showered where the beam struck.

Djana bolted. The robot swerved and bounded after her. It paid no attention to Flandry. And his shooting had no effect he could see.

Must be armored against energy beams—unlike the things we've met hitherto— He thumbed the power stud to full intensity. Fire cascaded blinding off the metal shape. Heedless, it bore down on his unarmed companion.

"Dodge toward me!" Flandry cried.

She heard and obeyed. The lance struck her from behind. It did not penetrate the air tank, as it would have the thinner cuirass of the spacesuit. The blow knocked her sprawling. She rolled over, scrambled up, and fled on. Wings beat. The machine was hopping around to get at her from the front.

It passed by Flandry. He leaped. His arms locked around the neck of the horsehead. He threw a leg over the body. The wings boomed behind him where he rode.

And still the thing did not fight him, still it chased Djana. But Flandry's mass slowed it, made it stumble. Twisting about, he fired into the right wing. Sheet metal and a rib gave way. Crippled, the robot went to the ground. It threshed and bucked. Somehow Flandry hung on. Battered, half stunned, he kept his blaster snout within centimeters of the head and the trigger held back. His faceplate darkened itself against furious radiance. Heat struck at him like teeth.

Abruptly came quiet. He had pierced through to an essential part and slain the killer.

He sprawled across it, gasping the oven-hot air into his mouth, aware of undergarments sodden with sweat and muscles athrob with bruises, dimly aware that he had better arise. Not until Djana returned to him did he feel able to.

A draught of water and a stimpill shoved through his

53

chowlock restored a measure of strength. He looked at the machine he had destroyed and thought vaguely that it was quite handsome. Like a dreamworld knight . . . Almost of themselves his arm lifted in salute and his voice murmured, "Ahoy, ahoy, check."

"What?" Djana asked, equally faintly.

"Nothing." Flandry willed the aches out of his consciousness and the shakes out of his body. "Let's get going."

"Y-y-yes." She was suffering worse from reaction than him. Her features seemed completely drained. She started off with mechanical strides, back toward the mountain.

"Wait a tick!" Flandry grabbed her shoulder. "Where're you bound?"

"Away," she said without tone. "Before something else comes after us."

"To sit in the sealtent—or at best, the boat—and wait for death? No, thanks." Flandry turned her about. She was too numbed to resist. "Here, swallow a booster of your own."

He had lost all but a rag of hope himself. The centrum was at the far side of the pattern, some ten kilometers hence. If robots were programed actually to attack humans, this close to where the great computer had been— *We'll explore a wee bit further, regardless. Why not?*

A machine appeared. At first it was a glint on the horizon, metal reflecting Mimirlight. Traveling fast across the plain, it gained shape within minutes. *Headed straight this way. And big!* Flandry cursed. Half dragging Djana, he made for a house-sized piece of meteoritic stone. From its top, defense might be possible.

The robot went past.

Djana sobbed her thanks. After a second, Flandry recovered from the shock of his latest deliverance. He stood where he was, holding the girl against him, and watched. The machine wasn't meant for combat. It was not much more than a self-operating flatbed truck with a pair of lifting arms.

It loaded the fallen lancer aboard and returned whence it came.

"For repairs," Flandry breathed. "No wonder we don't find stray parts in this neighborhood."

Djana shuddered in his arms.

His words went slowly on, shaping the thoughts they uttered: "Two classes of killer robot, then. One is free-ranging, fights indiscriminately, comes here to get fixed if it can make the trip, and doubtless returns to the wilderness for more hunting. While it's here, it keeps the peace.

"The other kind stays here, does fight here—though it doesn't interfere with the first kind or the maintenance machines—and is carefully salvaged when it comes to grief."

He shook his head in bewilderment. "I don't know if that's encouraging or not." Gazing down at Djana: "How do you feel?"

The drug he had forced on her was taking hold. It was not magical; it couldn't marshal resources which were no longer there. But for a time he and she would be alert, cool-headed, strong, quick-reacting. *And we'd better complete our business before the metabolic bill is presented,* Flandry recalled.

Her lips twitched in a woebegone smile. "I guess I'll do," she said. "Are you certain we should continue?"

"No. However, we will."

The next two squares they crossed were empty. One to their left was occupied. The humans kept a taut watch on that robot as they went past, but it did not stir. It was a tread-mounted cylinder, taller and broader than a man, its two arms ending in giant mauls, its head—the top of it, anyway, where there were what must be sensors—crowned with merlons like the battlements of some ancient tower. The sight jogged at Flandry's memory. An idea stirred in him but vanished before he could seize it. It could wait; readiness for another assault could not.

Djana startled him: "Nicky, does each of them stay inside its own square?"

"And defend that particular bit of territory against intruders?" Flandry's mind sprang. He smacked fist into palm. "By Jumbo, I think you're right! It could be a scheme for guarding the centrum . . . against really dangerous gizmos that don't behave themselves on this plain . . . a weird scheme, but then, everything on Wayland is weird. —Yes. The types of, uh, wild robot we've seen, and the ambulance and such, they're recognized as harmless and left alone. We don't fit into that program, so we're fair game."

"Not all the squares are occupied," she said dubiously.

He shrugged. "Maybe a lot of sentries are under repair at present." Excitement waxed in him. "The important point is, we can get across. Either directly across the lines, or over to a boundary and then around the whole layout. We simply avoid sections where any machine is. Making sure none are lurking behind a rock or whatever, of course." He hugged her. "Sweetheart, I do believe we're going to make it!"

The same eagerness kindled in her. They stepped briskly forth.

A figure that came into view, two kilometers ahead, as they passed the hillock which had concealed it, drew a cry from her. "Nicky, a man!" He jolted to a stop and raised his binoculars in unsteady hands. The object was indeed creepily similar to a large spacesuited human. But there were differences of detail, and it stood as death-still as the tower thing, and it was armed with sword and shield. Rather, its arms terminated in those pieces of war gear. Flandry lowered the glasses.

"No such luck," he said. "Not that it'd be luck. Anybody who's come here and taken charge like this would probably scupper us. It's yet another brand of guard robot." He tried to joke. "That means a further detour. I'm getting more exercise than I really want, aren't you?"

"You could destroy it."

"Maybe. Maybe not. If our friend the knight was typical, as I suspect, the lot of them are fairly well armored against energy beams. Besides, I don't care to waste charge. Used too bloody much in that last encounter. Another fracas, and we could be weaponless." Flandry started off on a slant across the square. "We'll avoid him and go catercorner past the domain of that comparatively mild-looking chap there."

Djana's gaze followed his finger. Remotely gleamed other immobile forms, including a duplicate of the hippoid and three of the anthropoid. Doubtless more were hidden by irregularities of terrain or its steep fall to the horizon. The machine which Flandry had in mind was closer, just left of his intended path. It was another cylinder, more tall and slim than the robot with the hammers. The smooth bright surface was unbroken by limbs. The conical head was partly split down the middle, above an array of instruments.

"He may simply be a watcher," Flandry theorized.

They had passed by, the gaunt abstract statue was falling behind, when Djana yelled.

Flandry spun about. The thing had left its square and was entering the one they were now in.

Dust and sparkling ice crystals whirled in the meter of space between its base and the ground. *Air cushion drive,* beat through Flandry. He looked frantically around for shelter. Nothing. This square held only basalt and frozen water.

"Run!" he cried. He retreated backward himself, blaster out. The heart slugged in him, the breath rasped, still hot from his prior battle.

A pencil of white fire struck at him from the cleft head. It missed at its range, but barely. He felt heat gust where the energy splashed and steam exploded. A sharp small thunderclap followed.

This kind does pack a gun!

Reflexively, he returned a shot. Less powerful, his beam bounced off the alloy hide. The robot moved on in. He could hear the roar of its motor. A direct hit at closer quarters would pierce his suit and body. He fired again and prepared to flee.

If I can divert that tin bastard— It did not occur to Flandry that his action might get him accused of gallantry. He started off in a different direction from the girl's. Longer-legged, he had a feebly better chance than she of keeping ahead of death, reaching a natural barricade and making a stand. . . .

Tensed with the expectation of lightning, the hope that his air unit would give protection and not be ruined, he had almost reached the next line when he realized there had been no fire. He braked and turned to stare behind.

The robot must have halted right after the exchange. Its top swung back and forth, as if in search. Surely it must sense him.

It started off after Djana.

Flandry spat an oath and pounded back to help. She had a good head start, but the machine was faster, and if it had crossed one line, wouldn't it cross another? Flandry's boots slammed upon stone. Oxygen-starved, his brain cast forth giddiness and patches of black. His intercepting course brought him nearer. He shot. The bolt went wild. He bounded yet more swiftly. Again he shot. This time he hit.

The robot slowed, veered as if to meet this antagonist who could be dangerous, faced away once more and resumed its pursuit of Djana. Flandry held down his trigger and hosed it with flame. The girl crossed the boundary. The robot stopped dead.

*But—but—*gibbered in Flandry's skull.

The robot stirred, lifted, and swung toward him. It moved hesitantly, wobbling a trifle, not as if damaged—it couldn't have been—but as if . . . puzzled?

I shouldn't be toting a blaster, Flandry thought in the turmoil. *With my shape, I'm supposed to carry sword and shield.*

57

The truth crashed into him.

He took no time to examine it. He knew simply that he must get into the same square as Djana. An anthropoid with blade and scute in place of hands could not crawl very well. Flandry went on all fours. He scuttled backward. The lean tall figure rocked after him, but no faster. Its limited computer—an artificial brain moronic and monomaniacal—could reach no decision as to what he was and what to do about him.

He crossed the line. The robot settled to the ground.

Flandry rose and tottered toward Djana. She had collapsed several meters away. He joined her. Murk spun down upon him.

It lifted in minutes, after his air unit purified the atmosphere in his suit and his stimulated cells drank the oxygen. He sat up. The machine that had chased them was retreating to the middle of the adjacent square, another gleam against the dark plain, under the dark sky. He looked at his blaster's charge indicator. It stood near zero. He could reload it from the powerpack he carried, but his life-support units needed the energy worse. Maybe.

Djana was rousing too. She half raised herself, fell across his lap, and wept. "It's no use, Nicky. We can't make it. We'll be murdered. And if we do get by, what'll we find? A thing that builds killing engines. Let's go back. We can go back the way we came. Can't we? And have a little, little while alive together—"

He consoled her until the chill and hardness of the rock on which he sat got through to him. Then, stiffly, he rose and assisted her to her feet. His voice sounded remote and strange in his ears. "Ordinarily I'd agree with you, dear. But I think I see what the arrangement is. The way the bishop behaved. Didn't you notice?"

"B-b-bishop?"

"Consider. Like the knight, I'm sure, the bishop attacks when the square he's on is invaded. I daresay the result of a move on this board depends on the outcome of the battle that follows it. Now a bishop can only proceed *offensively* along a diagonal. And the pieces are only programed to fight one other piece at a time: of certain kinds, at that." Flandry stared toward his hidden destination. "I imagine the anthropoids are the pawns. I wonder why. Maybe because they're the most numerous pieces, and the computer was lonely for mankind?"

"Computer?" She huddled against him.

"Has to be. Nothing else could have made this. It used the engineering facilities it had, possibly built some addi-

58

tional manufacturing plant. It didn't bother coloring the squares or the pieces, knowing quite well which was which. That's why I didn't see at once we're actually on a giant chessboard." Flandry grimaced. "If I hadn't . . . we'd've quit, returned, and died. Come on." He urged her forward.

"We can't go further," she pleaded. "We'll be set on."

"Not if we study the positions of the pieces," he said, "and travel on the squares that nobody can currently enter."

After some trudging: "My guess is, the computer split its attention into a number of parts. One or more to keep track of the wild robots. Two, with no intercommunication, to be rival chessmasters. That could be why it hasn't noticed something strange is going on today. I wonder if it can notice anything new any longer, without being nudged."

He zigzagged off the board with Djana, onto the blessed safe unmarked part of the land, and walked around the boundary. En route he saw a robot that had to be a king. It loomed four meters tall in the form of a man who wore the indoor dress of centuries ago, goldplated and crowned with clustered diamonds. It bore no weapons. He learned later that it captured by divine right.

They reached the ancient buildings. The worker machines that scuttled about had kept them in good repair. Flandry stopped before the main structure. He tuned his radio to standard frequency. "At this range," he said to that which was within, "you've got to have some receiver that'll pick up my transmission."

Code clicked and gibbered in his earplugs; and then, slowly, rustily, but gathering sureness as the words advanced, like the voice of one who has been heavily asleep: "Is . . . it . . . you? A man . . . returned at last? . . . No, two men, I detect—"

"More or less," Flandry said.

Across the plain, beasts and chessmen came to a halt.

"Enter. The airlock . . . Remove your spacesuits inside. It is Earth-conditioned, with . . . furnished chambers. Inspection reveals a supply of undeteriorated food and drink. . . . I hope you will find things in proper order. Some derangements are possible. The time was long and empty."

CHAPTER

X

Djana stumbled to bed and did not wake for thirty-odd hours. Flandry needed less rest. After breakfast he busied himself, languidly at first but with increasing energy. What he learned fascinated him so much that he regretted not daring to spend time exploring in depth the history of these past five centuries on Wayland.

He was in the main control room, holding technical discussions with the prime computer, when the speaker in its quaint-looking instrument bank said in its quaint-sounding Anglic: "As instructed, I have kept your companion under observation. Her eyelids are moving."

Flandry got up. "Thanks," he said automatically. It was hard to remember that no living mind flickered behind those meters and readout screens. An awareness did, yes, but not like that of any natural sophont, no matter how strange to man; this one was in some ways more and in some ways less than organic. "I'd better go to her. Uh, have a servitor bring hot soup and, uh, tea and buttered toast, soon's it can."

He strode down corridors silent except for the hum of machines, past apartments that held a few moldering possessions of men long dead, until he found hers.

"Nicky—" She blinked mistily and reached tremulous arms toward him. How thin and pale she'd grown! He could just hear her. Bending for a kiss, he felt her lips passive beneath his.

"Nicky . . . are we . . . all right?" The whisper-breath tickled his ear.

"Assuredly." He stroked her cheek. "Everything's on orbit."

"Outside?"

"Safe as houses. Safer than numerous houses I could name." Flandry straightened. "Relax. We'll start putting meat back on those lovely bones in a few minutes. By departure date, you ought to be completely yourself again."

She frowned, shook her head in a puzzled way, tried to sit up. "Hoy, not yet," he said, laying hands on the bare

60

slight shoulders. "I prescribe lots of bed rest. When you're strong enough to find that boring, I'll arrange for entertainment tapes to be projected. The computer says there're a few left. Ought to be interesting, a show that old."

Still she struggled feebly. The chemical-smelling air fluttered fast, in and out of her lungs. Alarm struck him. "What's the trouble, Djana?"

"I . . . don't know. Dizzy—"

"Oh, well. After what you've been through."

Cold fingers clutched his arm. "Nicky. This moon. Is it . . . worth . . . anything?"

"Huh?"

"Money!" she shrieked like an insect. "Is it worth money?"

Why should that make that much difference, right now? flashed through him. *Her past life's made her fanatical on the subject, I suppose, and—* "Sure."

"You're certain?" she gasped.

"My dear," he said, "Leon Ammon will have to work hard at it if he does *not* want to become one of the richest men in the Empire."

Her eyes rolled back till he saw only whiteness. She sagged in his embrace.

"Fainted," he muttered, and eased her down. Rising, scratching his scalp: "Computer, what kind of medical knowledge do you keep in your data banks?"

Reviving after a while, Djana sobbed. She wouldn't tell him why. Presently she was as near hysteria as her condition permitted. The computer found a sedative which Flandry administered.

On her next awakening she was calm, at any rate on the surface, but somehow remote from him. She answered his remarks so curtly as to make it clear she didn't want to talk. She did take nourishment, though. Afterward she lay frowning upward, fists clenched at her sides. He left her alone.

She was more cheerful by the following watch, and gradually reverted to her usual self.

But they saw scant of each other until they were again in space, bound back to the assigned round that was to end on Irumclaw where it began. She had spent most of the time previous in bed, waited on by robots while she recovered. He, vigor regained sooner, was preoccupied with setting matters on the moon to rights and supervising the repair of *Jake*. The latter job was complicated by the requirement that no clue remain to what had really taken place. He didn't want his superiors disbelieving his entries in the log concerning a malfunction of the hyperdrive oscillator which it had taken him three weeks to fix by himself.

Stark Wayland fell aft, and mighty Regin, and lurid Mimir; and the boat moved alone amidst a glory of stars. Flandry sat with Djana in the conn, which was the single halfway comfortable area to sit. Rested, clean, depilated, fed, liquored, in crisp coverall, breathing ample air, feeling the tug of a steady Terran *g* and the faint throb of the power that drove him toward his destination, he inhaled of a cigarette, patted Djana's hand, and grinned at her fresh-born comeliness. "Mission accomplished," he said. "I shall expect you to show your gratitude in the ways you know best."

"Well-l-l," she purred. After a moment: "How could you tell, Nicky?"

"Hm?"

"I don't yet understand what went wrong. You tried to explain before, but I was too dazed, I guess."

"Most simple," he said, entirely willing to parade his cleverness anew. "Once I saw we were caught in a chess game, everything else made sense. For instance, I remembered those radio masts being erected in the wilds. An impossible job unless the construction robots were free from attack. Therefore the ferocity of the roving machines was limited to their own kind. Another game, you see, with more potentialities and less predictability than chess, even the chess-cum-combat that had been developed when the regular sort got boring. New types of killer were produced at intervals and sent forth to see how they'd do against the older models. Our boat, and later we ourselves, were naturally taken for such newcomers; the robots weren't supplied with information about humans, and line-of-sight radio often had them out of touch with the big computer."

"When we tried to call for help, though—"

"You mean from the peak of Mt. Maidens? Well, obviously none of the wild robots would recognize our signal, on the band they used. And that part of the computer's attention which 'listened in' on its children simply filtered out my voice, the way you or I can fail to hear sounds when we're busy with something else. With so much natural static around, that's not surprising.

"Those masts were constructed strictly as relays for the robots—for the high frequencies which carried the digital transmissions—so that's why they didn't buck on my calls on any other band. The computer always did keep a small

62

part of itself on the *qui vive* for a voice call on standard frequencies. But it assumed that, if and when humans came back, they would descend straight from the zenith and land near the buildings as they used to. Hence it didn't make arrangements to detect people radio from any other direction."

Flandry puffed. Smoke curled across the viewscreen, as if to veil off the abysses beyond. "Maybe it should have done so, in theory," he said. "However, after all those centuries, the poor thing was more than a little bonkers. Actually, what it did—first establish that chess game, then modify it, then produce fighters that obeyed no rules, then extend the range and variety of their battles further and further across the moon—that was done to save most of its sanity."

"What?" Djana said, surprised.

"Why, sure. A thinking capability like that, with nothing but routine to handle, no new input, decade after decade—" Flandry shivered. "Br-rr! You must know what sensory deprivation does to organic sophonts. Our computer rescued itself by creating something complicated and unpredictable to watch." He paused before adding slyly: "I refrain from suggesting analogies to the Creator you believe in."

And regretted it when she bridled and snapped, "I want a full report on how you influenced the situation."

"Oh, for the best, for the best," he said. "Not that that was hard. The moment I woke the White King up, the world he'd been dreaming of came to an end." His metaphor went over her head, so he merely continued: "The computer's pathetically impatient to convert back to the original style of operations. Brother Ammon will find a fortune in metals waiting for his first ship.

"I do think you are morally obliged to recommend me for a substantial bonus, which he is morally obliged to pay."

"Morally!" The bitterness of a life which had never allowed her a chance to consider such questions whipped forth. But it seemed to him she exaggerated it, as if to provide herself an excuse for attacking. "Who are you to blat about morals, Dominic Flandry, who took an oath to serve the Empire and a bribe to serve Leon Ammon?"

Stung, he threw back: "What else could I do?"

"Refuse." Her mood softened. She shook her amber-locked head, smiled a sad smile, and squeezed his hand. "No, never mind. That would be too much to expect of anyone nowadays, wouldn't it? Let's be corrupt together,

Nicky darling, and kind to each other till we have to say goodbye."

He looked long at her, and at the stars, where his gaze remained, before he said quietly, "I suppose I can tell you what I've had in mind. I'll take the pay because I can use it; also the risk, for the rest of my life, of being found out and broken. It seems a reasonable price for holding a frontier."

Her lips parted. Her eyes widened. "I don't follow you."

"Irumclaw was due to be abandoned," he said. "Everybody knows—knew—it was. Which made the prophecy self-fulfilling: The garrison turned incompetent. The able civilians withdrew, taking their capital with them. Defensibility and economic value spiraled down toward the point where it really wouldn't be worth our rational while to stay. In the end, the Empire would let Irumclaw go. And without this anchor, it'd have to pull the whole frontier parsecs back; and Merseia and the Long Night would draw closer."

He sighed. "Leon Ammon is evil and contemptible," he went on. "Under different circumstances, I'd propose we gut him with a butterknife. But he does have energy, determination, actual courage and foresight of sorts.

"I went to his office to learn his intentions. When he told me, I agreed to go along because—well—

"If the Imperial bureaucrats were offered Wayland, they wouldn't know what to do with it. Probably they'd stamp its existence Secret, to avoid making any decisions or laying out any extra effort. If nothing else, a prize like that would make 'conciliation and consolidation' a wee bit difficult, eh?

"Ammon, though, he's got a personal profit to harvest. He'll go in to stay. His enterprise will be a *human* one. He'll make it pay off so well—he'll get so much economic and thereby political leverage from it—that he can force the government to protect his interests. Which means standing fast on Irumclaw. Which means holding this border, and even extending control a ways outward.

"In short," Flandry concluded, "as the proverb phrases it, he may be a son of a bitch, but he's our son of a bitch."

He stubbed out the cigarette with a violent gesture and turned back to the girl, more in search of forgetfulness than anything else.

Strangely, in view of the fellow-feeling she had just shown him, she did not respond. Her hands fended him off. The blue glance was troubled upon his. "Please, Nicky. I want to think . . . about what you've told me."

He respected her wish and relaxed in his seat, crossing shank over knee. "I daresay I can contain myself for a bit." The sight of her mildened the harshness that had risen in him. He chuckled. "Be warned, it won't be a long bit. You're too delectable."

Her mouth twitched, but not in any smile. "I never realized such things mattered to you," she said uncertainly.

Having been raised to consider idealism gauche, he shrugged. "They'd better. I live in the Terran Empire."

"But if—" She leaned forward. "Do you seriously believe, Nicky, Wayland can make that big a difference?"

"I like to believe it. Why do you ask? I can't well imagine you giving a rusty horntoot about future generations."

"That's what I mean. Suppose . . . Nicky, suppose, oh, something happens so Leon doesn't get to exploit Wayland. So nobody does. How'd that affect us—you and me?"

"Depends on our lifespans, I'd guess, among other items. Maybe we'd see no change. Or maybe, twenty-thirty years hence, we'd see the Empire retreat the way I was talking about."

"But that wouldn't mean its end!"

"No, no. Not at once. We could doubtless finish our lives in the style to which we want to become accustomed." Flandry considered. "Or could we? Political repercussions at home . . . unrest leading to upheaval . . . well, I don't know."

"We could always find ourselves a safe place. A nice offside colony planet—not so offside it's primitive, but—"

"Yes, probably." Flandry scowled. "I don't understand what's gnawing you. We'll report to Ammon and that will finish our part. Remember, he's holding the rest of our pay."

She nodded. For a space they were both silent. The stars in the viewscreen made an aureole behind her gold head.

Then craftiness came upon her, and she smiled and murmured: "It wouldn't make any difference, would it, if somebody else on Irumclaw—somebody besides Leon—got Wayland. Would it?"

"I guess not, if you mean one of his brother entrepreneurs." Flandry's unease waxed. "What're you thinking of, wench? Trying to rake in more for yourself, by passing the secret on to a competitor? I wouldn't recommend that. Bloody dripping dangerous."

"You—"

"Emphatically not! I'll squirrel away my money, and for

the rest of my Irumclaw tour, you won't believe what a good boy I'll be. No more Old Town junkets whatsoever; wholesome on-base recreation and study of naval manuals. Fortunately, my Irumclaw tour is nearly done."

Flandry captured her hands in his. "I won't even risk seeing you," he declared. "Nor should you take any avoidable chances. The universe would be too poor without you."

Her lips pinched together. "If that's how you feel—"

"It is." Flandry leered. "Fortunately, we've days and days before we arrive. Let's use them, hm-m-m?"

Her eyes dropped, and rose, and she was on his lap embracing him, warm, soft, smiling, pupils wide between the long lashes, and "Hm-m-m indeed," she crooned.

Thunder ended a dream. Nothingness.

He woke, and wished he hadn't. Someone had scooped out his skull to make room for the boat's nuclear generator.

No . . . He tried to roll over, and couldn't.

When he groaned, a hand lifted his head. Cool wetness touched his mouth. "Drink this," Djana's voice told him from far away.

He got down a couple of tablets with the water, and could look around him. She stood by the bunk, staring down. As the stimpills took hold and the pain receded, her image grew less blurred, until he could identify the hardness that sat on her face. Craning his neck, he made out that he lay on his back with wrists and ankles wired—securely—to the bunkframe.

"Feel better?" Her tone was flat.

"I assume you gave me a jolt from your stun gun after I feel asleep," he succeeded in croaking.

"I'm sorry, Nicky." Did her shell crack the tiniest bit, for that tiniest instant?

"What's the reason?"

She told him about Rax, ending: "We're already bound for the rendezvous. If I figured right, remembering what you taught me, it's about forty or fifty light-years; and I set the 'pilot for top cruising hyperspeed, the way you said I ought to."

He was too groggy for the loss of his fortune to seem more than academic. But dismay struck through him like a blunt nail. "Four or five days! With me trussed up?"

"I'm sorry," she repeated. "I don't dare give you a chance to grab me or—or anything—" She hesitated. "I'll

66

take care of you as best I can. Nothing personal in this. You know? It's that million credits."

"What makes you think your unknown friends will honor their end of the deal?"

"If Wayland's what you say, a megacredit's going to be a microbe to them. And I can keep on being useful till I leave them." All at once, it was as if a sword spoke: "That payment will make me my own."

Flandry surrendered to his physical misery.

Which passed. But was followed by the miseries of confinement. He couldn't do most isometric exercises. The wires would have cut him. A few were possible; and he spent hours flexing what muscles he was able to; and Djana was fairly good about massaging him. Nonetheless he ached and tingled.

Djana also kept her promise to give him a nurse's attentions. Hers weren't the best, for lack of training and equipment, but they served. And she read to him by the hour, over the intercom, from the bookreels he had along. She even offered to make love to him. On the third day he accepted.

Otherwise little passed between them: the constraints were too many for conversation. They spent most of their time separately, toughing it out. Once he was over the initial shock and had disciplined himself, Flandry didn't do badly at first. While no academician, he had many experiences, ideas, and stray pieces of information to play with. Toward the end, though, environmental impoverishment got to him and each hour became a desert century. When at last the detectors buzzed, he had to struggle out of semi-delirium to recognize what the noise was. When the outercom boomed with words, he blubbered for joy.

But when hypervelocities were matched and phasing in was completed and airlocks were joined and the other crew came aboard, Djana screamed.

CHAPTER
XI

The Merseians treated him correctly if coolly. He was unbound, conducted aboard their destroyer, checked by a physician experienced in dealing with foreign species, given a chance to clean and bestir himself. His effects were returned, with the natural exception of weapons. A cubbyhole was found and curtained off for him and the girl. Food was brought them, and the toilet facilities down the passage were explained for her benefit. A guard was posted, but committed no molestation. Prisoners could scarcely have been vouchsafed more on this class of warcraft; and the time in space would not be long.

Djana kept keening, "I thought they were human, I thought they were human, only an-an-another damn gang —" She clung to him. "What'll they do with us?"

"I can't say," he replied with no measurable sympathy, "except that I don't imagine they care to have us take home our story."

A story of an intelligence ring on Irumclaw, headed by that Rax—whose planet of origin is doubtless in the Roidhunate, not the Empire—and probably staffed by members of the local syndicates. Not to mention the fact that apparently there is a Merseian base in the wilderness, this close to our borders. A crawling went along his spine. *Then too, when word gets back to their headquarters, somebody may well want a personal interview with me.*

The destroyer grappled the spaceboat alongside and started off. Flandry tried to engage his guard in conversation, but the latter had orders to refrain. The one who brought dinner did agree to convey a request for him. Flandry was surprised when it was granted: that he might observe approach and landing. *Though why not? To repeat, they won't return me to blab what I've seen.*

Obviously the destination coordinates that Rax had given Djana meant the boat would be on a course bringing her within detection range of a picket ship; and any such wouldn't go far from the base. Flandry got his summons in two or three hours. He left Djana knotted around her wretchedness—*serves her right, the stupid slut!*—and preceded his armed guide forward.

The layout resembled that of a human vessel. Details varied, to allow for variations in size, shape, language, and culture. Yet it was the same enclosing metal narrowness, the same drone and vibration, the same warm oily-smelling gusts from ventilator grilles, the same duties to perform.

But the crew were big, green-skinned, hairless, spined and tailed. Their outfits were black, of foreign cut and drape, belts holding war knives. They practiced rituals and deferences—a gesture, a word, a stepping aside—with the smoothness of centuried tradition. The glimpses of something personal, a picture or souvenir, showed a taste more austere and abstract than was likely in a human space-hand. The body odors that filled this crowded air were sharper and, somehow, drier than man's. The dark eyes that followed him had no whites.

Broch—approximately, Second Mate—Tryntaf the Tall greeted him in the chartroom. "You are entitled to the courtesies, Lieutenant. True, you are under arrest for violation of ensovereigned space; but our realms are not at war."

"I thank the *broch*," Flandry said in his best Eriau, complete with salute of gratitude. He refrained from adding that, among other provisions, the Covenant of Alfzar enjoined both powers from claiming territory in the buffer zone. Surely here, as on Starkad and elsewhere, a "mutual assistance pact" had been negotiated with an amenable, or cowed, community of autochthons.

He was more interested in what he saw. Belike he looked on his deathplace.

The viewport displayed the usual stars, so many as to be chaos to the untrained perception. Flandry had learned the tricks—strain out the less bright through your lashes; find your everywhere-visible markers, like the Magellanic Clouds; estimate by its magnitude the distance of the nearest giant, Betelgeuse. He soon found that he didn't need them for a guess at where he was. Early in the game he'd gotten Djana to recite those coordinates for him and stored them in his memory; and the sun disc he saw was of a type uncommon enough, compared to the red dwarf majority, that only one or two would exist in any given neighborhood.

The star was, in fact, akin to Mimir—somewhat less massive and radiant, but of the same furious whiteness, with the same boiling spots and leaping prominences. It

69

must be a great deal older, though, for it had no surrounding nebulosity. At its distance, it showed about a third again the angular diameter of Sol seen from Terra.

"F5," Tryntaf said, "mass 1.34, luminosity 3.06, radius 1.25." The standard to which he referred was, in reality, his home sun, Korych; but Flandry recalculated the values in Solar terms with drilled-in ease. "We call it Siekh. The planet we are bound for we call Talwin."

"Ah." The man nodded. "And what more heroes of your Civil Wars have you honored?"

Tryntaf threw him a sharp glance. *Damn, I forgot again*, he thought. *Always make the opposition underestimate you.* "I am surprised at your knowledge of our history before the Roidhunate, Lieutenant," the Merseian said. "But then, considering that our pickets were ordered to watch for a Terran scout, the pilot must be of special interest."

"Oh, well," Flandry said modestly.

"To answer your question, few bodies here are worth naming. Swarms of asteroids, yes, but just four true planets, the smallest believed to be a mere escaped satellite. Orbits are wildly skewed and eccentric. Our astronomers theorize that early in the life of this system, another star passed through, disrupting the normal configuration."

Flandry studied the world growing before him. The ship had switched from hyperdrive to sublight under gravs—so few KPS as to support the idea of many large meteoroids. (They posed no hazard to a vessel which could detect them in plenty of time to dodge, or could simply let them bounce off a forcefield; but they would jeopardize the career of a skipper who thus inelegantly wasted power.) Talwin's crescent, blinding white, blurred along the edges, indicated that, like Venus, it was entirely clouded over. But it was not altogether featureless; spots and bands of red could be seen.

"Looks none too promising," he remarked. "Aren't we almighty close to the sun?"

"The planet is," Tryntaf said. "It is late summer—everywhere; there is hardly any axial tilt—and temperatures remain fierce. Dress lightly before you disembark, Lieutenant! At periastron, Talwin comes within 0.87 astronomical units of Siekh; but apastron is at a full 2.62 a.u."

Flandry whistled. "That's as eccentic as I can remember ever hearing of in a planet, if not more. Uh . . . about one-half, right?" He saw a chance to appear less than a genius. "How can you survive? I mean, a good big axial tilt would protect one hemisphere, at least, from the worst

70

effects of orbital extremes. But this ball, well, any life it may have has got to be unlike yours or mine."

"Wrong," was Tryntaf's foreseeable reply. "Atmosphere and hydrosphere moderate the climate to a degree; likewise location. Those markings you see are of biological origin, spores carried into the uppermost air. Photosynthesis maintains a breathable oxynitrogen mixture."

"Uh-h-h . . . diseases?" *No, wait, now you're acting too stupid. True, what's safe for a Merseian isn't necessarily so for a man. We may have extraordinarily similar biochemistries, but still, we've fewer bugs in common that are dangerous to us than we have with our respective domestic animals. By the same token, though, a world as different as Talwin isn't going to breed anything that'll affect us . . . at least, nothing that'll produce any syndrome modern medicine can't easily slap down. Tryntaf knows I know that much.* The thought had flashed through Flandry in part of a second. "I mean allergens and other poisons."

"Some. They cause no serious trouble. The bioform is basically akin to ours, L-amino proteins in water solution. Deviations are frequent, of course. But you or I could survive awhile on native foods, if we chose them with care. Over an extended period we would need dietary supplements. They have been compounded for emergency use."

Flandry decided that Tryntaf lacked any sense of humor. Most Merseians had one, sometimes gusty, sometimes cruel, often incomprehensible to men. He had in his turn baffled various of them when he visited their planet; even after he put a joke into their equivalents, they did not see why it should be funny that one diner said, *"Bon appetit"* and the other said, "Ginsberg."

Sure. They differ, same as us. My life could depend on the personality of the commandant down there. Will I be able to recognize any chance he might give me?

He sought to probe his companion, but was soon left alone on grounds of work to do, except for the close-mouthed rating who tail-sat by the door.

Watching the view took his mind partly off his troubles. He could pick up visual clues that a layman would be blind to, identify what they represented, and conclude what the larger pattern must be.

Talwin had no moon—maybe once, but not after the invader star had virtually wrecked this system. Flandry did see two relay satellites glint, in positions indicating they belonged to a synchronous triad. If the Merseians had installed no more than that, they had a barebones base here.

It was what you'd expect at the end of this long a communications line: a watchpost, a depot, a first-stage receiving station for reports from border-planet agents like Rax.

Aside from their boss, those latter wouldn't have been told Siekh's coordinates, or of its very existence. They'd have courier torpedoes stashed away in the hinterland, target preset and clues to the target removed. Given elementary precautions, no Imperial loyalist was likely to observe the departure of one. Replenishment would be more of a problem, dependent on smuggling, but not overly difficult when the Terran service was undermanned and lax. Conveyance of fresh orders to the agents was no problem at all; who noticed what mail or what visitors drifted into Rax's dope shop?

The value of Talwin was obvious. Besides surveillance, it allowed closer contact with spies than would otherwise be possible. Flandry wondered if his own corps ran an analogous operation out Roidhunate way. Probably not. The Merseians were too vigilant, the human government too inert, its wealthier citizens too opposed to pungling up the cost of positive action.

Flandry shook himself, as if physically to cast off apprehension and melancholy, and concentrated on what he saw.

Clearances given and path computed, the destroyer dropped in a spiral that took her around the planet. Presumably her track was designed to avoid storms. Cooler air, moving equatorward from the poles, must turn summer into a "monsoon" season. Considering input energy, atmospheric pressure (which Tryntaf had mentioned was twenty percent greater than Terran), and rotation period (a shade over eighteen hours, he had said), weather surely got more violent here than ever at Home; and a long, thin, massive object like a destroyer was more vulnerable to wind than you might think.

Water vapor rose high before condensing into clouds. Passing over dayside below those upper layers, Flandry got a broad view.

A trifle smaller (equatorial diameter 0.97) and less dense than Terra, Talwin in this era had but a single continent. Roughly wedge-shaped, it reached from the north-pole area with its narrow end almost on the equator. Otherwise the land consisted of islands. While multitudinous, in the main they were thinly scattered.

Flandry guessed that the formation and melting of huge icecaps in the course of the twice-Terran year disturbed isostatic balance. Likewise, the flooding and great rainstorms of summer, the freezing of winter, would speed erosion and hence the redistribution of mass. Tectony must proceed at a furious rate; earthquake, vulcanism, the sinking of old land and the rising of new, must be geologically common occurrences.

He made out one mountain range, running east-west along the 400-kilometer width of the continent near its middle. Those peaks dwarfed the Himalayas but were snowless, naked rock. Elsewhere, elevations were generally low, rounded, worn. North of the wall, the country seemed to be swamp. *Whew! That means in winter the icecap grows down to 45 degrees latitude! The glaciers grind everything flat.* The far southlands were a baked desolation, scoured by hurricanes. Quite probably, at midsummer lakes and rivers there didn't simply dry up, they boiled; and the equatorial ocean became a biological fence. It would be intriguing to know how evolution had diverged in the two hemispheres.

Beyond the sterile tropics, life not long ago had been outrageously abundant, jungle choking the central zone, the arctic abloom with low-growing plants. Now annual drought was taking its toll in many sections, leaves withering, stems crumbling, fires running wild, bald black patches of desiccation and decay. But other districts, especially near the coasts, got enough rain yet. Immense herds of grazers were visible on open ground; wings filled the air; shoal waters were darkened by weeds and swimmers. Most islands remained similarly fecund.

The dominant color of vegetation was blue, in a thousand shades—the photosynthetic molecule not chlorophyll, then, though likely to be a close chemical relative—but there were the expected browns, reds, yellows, the unexpected and stingingly Homelike splashes of green.

Descending, trailing a thunderclap, the ship crossed nightside. Flandry used photomultiplier and infrared step-up controls to go on with his watching. It confirmed the impressions he had gathered by day.

And the ship was back under the hidden sun, low, readying for setdown. Her latitude was about 40 degrees. In the north, the lesser members of the giant range gave way to foothills of their own. Flandry made out one volcano in that region, staining heaven with smoke. A river flowed thence, cataracting through canyons until it became broad and placid in the wooded plains further south. The diffuse light made it shine dully, like lead, on its track through yonder azure lands. Finally it ran out in a kilometers-wide bay.

The greenish-gray sea creamed white with surf along much of the coast. The tidal pull of Siekh in summer approximated that of Luna and Sol on Terra, and ocean currents flowed strongly. For some distance inland, dried, cracked, salt-streaked mud was relieved only by a few tough plant species adapted to it.

Uh-huh, Flandry reflected. *In spring the icecaps melt. Sea level rises by many meters. Storms get really stiff; they, and increasing tides, drive the waves in, over and over, to meet the floods running down from the mountains. . . . And Djana believes in a God Who gives a damn?*

Or should I say, Who gives a blessing?

He rubbed his cheek, observing with what exquisite accuracy nerves recorded pressure, texture, warmth, location, motion. *Well,* he thought, *I must admit, if Anyone's been in charge of my existence, He's furnished it with noble pleasures.* Despite everything, fear knocked in his heart and dried his mouth. *He's not about to take them away, is He? Not now! Later, when I'm old, when I don't really care, all right; but not now!*

He remembered comrades in arms who didn't make it as far through time as he'd done. That was no consolation, but rallied him. They hadn't whined.

And maybe something would turn up.

The scene tilted. The engines growled on a deeper note. The ship was landing.

The Merseian base stood on a bluff overlooking the river, thirty or so kilometers north of its mouth, well into fertile territory. The spaceport was minute, the facilities in proportion, as Flandry had surmised; nothing fancier than a few destroyers and lesser craft could work out of here. But he noticed several buildings within the compound that didn't seem naval.

Hm. Do the Merseians have more than one interest in Talwin? . . . I imagine they do at that. Otherwise they'd find a more hospitable planet for their base—or else a better-camouflaged one, say a sunless rogue. . . . You know, their intelligence activities here begin to look almost like an afterthought.

The ship touched down. Air pressure had gradually been raised during descent to match sea-level value. When interior gravity was cut off, the planet's reasserted itself and Flandry felt lighter. He gauged weight at nine-tenths or a hair less.

Tryntaf reappeared, issued an order, and redisappeared. Flandry was escorted to the lock. Djana waited by her

74

own guard. She seemed incredibly tiny and frail against the Merseian, a porcelain doll. "Nicky," she stammered, reaching toward him, "Nicky, please forgive me, please be good to me. I don't even know what they're saying."

"Maybe I will later," he snapped, "if they leave me in shape to do it."

She covered her eyes and shrank back. He regretted his reaction. She'd been suckered—by her cupidity; nonetheless, suckered—and the feel of her hand in his would have eased his isolation. But pride would not let him soften.

The lock opened. The gangway extruded. The prisoners were gestured out.

Djana staggered. Flandry choked. *Judas on a griddle, I was warned to change clothes and I forgot!*

The heat enveloped him, entered him, became him and everything else which was. Temperature could not be less than 80 Celsius—might well be higher—20 degrees below the Terran-pressure boiling point of water. A furnace wind roared dully across the ferrocrete, which wavered in his seared gaze. He was instantly covered, permeated, not with honest sweat but with the sliminess that comes when humidity reaches an ultimate. Breathing was like drowning.

Noises came loud to his ears through that dense air: wind, voices, clatter of machines. Odors borne from the jungle were pungent and musky, with traces of sulfurous reek. He saw a building blocky against the clouds, and on its roof a gong to call for prayers to the God of a world two and a half light-centuries hence. The shadowless illumination made distances hard to gauge; was that air-conditioned interior as remote as he dreaded?

The crew were making for it. They weren't in formation, but discipline lived in their close ranks and careful jog-trot. What Merseians had tasks to do outside wore muffling white coveralls with equipment on the back.

"Move along, Terran," said Flandry's guard. "Or do you enjoy our weather?"

The man started off. "I've known slightly more comfortable espresso cookers," he answered; but since the guard had never heard of espresso, or coffee for that matter, his repartee fell flat again.

CHAPTER
XII

In the Spartan tradition of Vach lords, the office of
Ydwyr the Seeker lacked any furniture save desk and cabinets. Though he and Morioch Sun-in-eye were seated, it
was on feet and tails, which looked to a human as if they
were crouched to spring. That, and their size, great even
for Wilwidh Merseians, and faint but sharp body odors,
and rumbling bass tones, and the explosive gutturals of
Eriau, gave Djana a sense of anger that might break loose
in slaughter. She could see that Flandry was worried and
caught his hand in the cold dampness of hers. He made no
response; standing rigid, he listened.

"Perhaps the *datholch* has been misinformed about this
affair," Morioch said with strained courtesy. Flandry
didn't know what the title signified—and Merseian grades
were subtle, variable things—but it was plainly a high one,
since the aristocratic-deferential form of address was used.

"I shall hearken to whatever the *qanryf* wishes to say,"
Ydwyr replied, in the same taut manner but with the
merely polite verbal construction. Flandry would have understood *"qanryf"* (the first letter representing, more or
less, *k* followed by *dh* = voiced *th*) from the argent saltire on Morioch's black uniform, had he not met the word
often before. Morioch was the commandant of this base,
or anyhow of its naval aspect; but the base was a minor
one.

He—stockily built, hard of features, incongruous
against the books and reelboxes whose shelves filled every
available square centimeter of wall space—declared: "This
is no capture of a scout who simply chanced by. The female alone should . . . unquestionably does tell the *datholch* that. But I didn't want to intrude on your work by
speaking to you of mine. Besides, since it's confidential,
the fewer who are told, the better. Correct?"

No guards had come in with their chief. They waited
beyond the archway curtains, which were not too soundproof to pass a cry for help. Opposite, seen through a window, waited Talwin's lethal summer. Blue-black and enor-

mous, a thunderhead was piling up over the stockade, where the banners of those Vachs and regions that had members here whipped on their staffs.

Ydwyr's mouth drew into thinner lines. "*I* could have been trusted," he said. Flandry didn't believe that mere wounded vanity spoke. Had a prerogative been infringed? What was Ydwyr?

He wore a gray robe without emblems; at its sash hung only a purse. He was taller than Morioch, but lean, wrinkled, aging. At first he had spoken softly, when the humans were brought before him from their quarters—on his demand after he learned of their arrival. As soon as the commandant had given him a slight amount of back talk, he had stiffened, and power fairly blazed from him.

Morioch confronted it stoutly. "That needs no utterance," he said. "I hope the *datholch* accepts that I saw no reason to trouble you with matters outside your own purposes here."

"Does the *qanryf* know every conceivable limit of my purposes?"

"No . . . however—" Rattled but game, Morioch redonned formality. "May I explain everything to the *datholch?*"

Ydwyr signed permission. Morioch caught a breath and commenced:

"When the *Brythioch* stopped by, these months agone, her chief intelligence officer gave me a word that did not then seem very interesting. You recall she'd been at Irumclaw, the Terran frontier post. There a *mei*—I have his name on record but don't remember it—had come on a scoutship pilot he'd met previously. The pilot, the male before you here, was running surveillance as part of his training for their Intelligence Corps. Normally that'd have meant nothing—standard procedure of theirs—but this particular male had been on Merseia in company with a senior Terran agent. Those two got involved in something which is secret from me but, I gather, caused major trouble to the Roidhunate. Protector Brechdan Ironrede was said to have been furious."

Ydwyr started. Slowly he lifted one bony green hand and said, "You have not told me the prisoner's name."

"Let the *datholch* know this is Junior Lieutenant Dominic Flandry."

Silence fell, except for the wind whose rising skirl began to pierce the heavily insulated walls. Ydwyr's gaze probed and probed. Djana whispered frantic, repeated prayers.

77

Flandry felt the sweat slide down his ribs. He needed all his will to hold steady.

"Yes," Ydwyr said at last, "I have heard somewhat about him."

"Then the *datholch* may appreciate this case more than I do," Morioch said, looking relieved. "To be honest, I knew nothing of Flandry till the *Brythioch*—"

"Continue your account," Ydwyr said unceremoniously.

Morioch's relief vanished, but he plowed on: "As the *datholch* wishes. Whatever the importance of Flandry himself—he appears a cub to me—he was associated with this other agent . . . *khraich,* yes, it comes back . . . Max Abrams. And Abrams was, is, definitely a troublemaker of the worst sort. Flandry appears to be a *protégé* of his. Perhaps, already, an associate? Could his assignment to Irumclaw involve more than showed on the skin?

"This much the *mei* reported to the chief intelligence officer of his ship. The officer, in turn, directed our agents in the city"—*Rax, of course, and those in Rax's pay,* Flandry thought through the loudening wind—"to keep close watch on this young male. If he did anything unusual, it should be investigated as thoroughly as might be.

"The officer asked me to stand by. As I've said, nothing happened for months, until I'd almost forgotten. We get so many leads that never lead anywhere in intelligence work.

"But lately a courier torpedo arrived. The message was that Flandry was collaborating closely but, apparently, secretly, with the leader of an underworld gang. The secrecy is understandable—ultra-illegal behavior—and our agent's first guess was that normal corruption was all that was involved." Scorn freighted Morioch's voice. "However, following orders, they infiltrated the operation. They learned what it was."

He described Wayland, to the extent of Ammon's knowledge, and Ydwyr nodded. "Yes," the old Merseian said, "I understand. The planet is too far from home to be worth our while—at present—but it is not desirable that Terrans reoccupy it."

"Our Irumclaw people are good," Morioch said. "They had to make a decision and act on their own. Their plan succeeded. Does the *datholch* agree they should get extra reward?"

"They had better," Ydwyr said dryly, "or they might decide Terrans are more generous masters. You have yet to tell them to eliminate those who know about the lost planet, correct?— Well, but what did they do?"

"The *datholch* sees this female. After Flandry had investigated the planet, she captured him and brought his boat to a section where our pickets were bound to detect it."

"Hun-n-nh . . . is she one of ours?"

"No, she thought she was working for a rival human gang. But the *datholch* may agree she shows a talent for that kind of undertaking."

Flandry couldn't help it, too much compassion welled through his despair, he bent his head down toward Djana's and muttered: "Don't be afraid. They're pleased with what you did for them. I expect they'll pay you something and let you go."

To spy on us—driven by blackmail as well as money— but you can probably vanish into the inner Empire. Or . . . maybe you'd like the work. Your species never treated you very kindly.

"And that is the whole tale, *qanryf?*" Ydwyr asked.

"Yes," Morioch said. "Now the *datholch* sees the importance. Bad enough that we had to capture a boat. That'll provoke a widespread search, which might stumble on places like Talwin. The odds are against it, true, and we really had no choice. But we cannot release Flandry."

"I did not speak of that," Ydwyr said, cold again. "I did, and do, want both these beings in my custody."

"But—"

"Do you fear they may escape?"

"No. Certainly not. But the *datholch* must know . . . the value of this prisoner as a subject for interrogation—"

"The methods your folk would use would leave him of no value for anything else," Ydwyr rapped. "And he can't have information we don't already possess; I assume the Intelligence Corps is not interested in his private life. He is here only through a coincidence."

"Can the *datholch* accept that strong a coincidence? Flandry met the *mei* by chance, yes. But that he, of every possible pilot, went off to the lost planet as a happenstance: to that I must say no."

"I say yes. He is precisely the type to whom such things occur. If one exposes oneself to life, *qanryf,* life will come to one. I have my own uses for him and will not see him ruined. I also want to learn more about this female. They go into my keeping."

Morioch flushed and well-nigh roared: "The *datholch* forgets that Flandry worked tail-entwined with Abrams to thwart the Protector!"

Ydwyr lifted a hand, palm down, and chopped it across his breast. Flandry sucked in a breath. That gesture was seldom used, and never by those who did not have the hereditary right. Morioch swallowed, bent head above folded hands, and muttered, "I beg the *datholch's* forgiveness." Merseians didn't often beg, either.

"Granted," Ydwyr said. "Dismissed."

"Kh-h . . . the *datholch* understands I must report this to headquarters, with what recommendations my duty demands I make?"

"Certainly. I shall be sending messages of my own. No censure will be in them." Ydwyr's hauteur vanished. Though his smile was not a man's, but only pulled the upper lip back off the teeth, Flandry recognized friendliness. "Hunt well, Morioch Sun-in-eye."

"I thank . . . and wish a good hunt . . . to you." Morioch rose, saluted, and left.

Outside, the sky had gone altogether black. Lightning flamed, thunder bawled, wind yammered behind galloping sheets of rain, whose drops smoked back off the ground. Djana fell into Flandry's arms; they upheld each other.

Releasing her, he turned to Ydwyr and made the best Merseian salute of honor which a human could. "The *datholch* is thanked with my whole spirit," he said in Eriau.

Ydwyr smiled anew. The overhead fluoropanel, automatically brightening as the storm deepened, made the room into a warm little cave. (Or a cool one; that rain was not far below its boiling point.) The folds in his robe showed him relaxing. "Be seated if you desire," he invited.

The humans were quick to accept, lowering themselves to the rubbery floor and leaning back against a cabinet. Their knees were grateful. To be sure, there was a psychological drawback; now Ydwyr loomed over them like a heathen god.

But I'm not going to be drugged, brainscrubbed, or shot. Not today. Maybe . . . maybe, eventually, an exchange deal . . .

Ydwyr had returned to dignified impassivity. *I mustn't keep him waiting.* Strength seeped back into Flandry's cells. He said, "May I ask the *datholch* to tell me his standing, in order that I can try to show him his due honor?"

"We set most ritual aside—of necessity—in my group here," the Merseian answered. "But I am surprised that one who speaks Eriau fluently and has been on our home planet has not encountered the term before."

"The uh, the *datholch*—may I inform the *datholch*, his language was crammed into me in tearing haste; my stay

80

on his delightful world was brief; and what I was taught at the Academy dealt mainly with—uh—"

"I told you the simple forms of respect will do on most occasions." Ydwyr's smile turned downward this time, betokening a degree of grimness. "And I know how you decided not to end your sentence. Your education dealt with us primarily as military opponents." He sighed. *"Khraich,* I don't fear the tactless truth. We Merseians have plenty of equivalents of you, the God knows. It's regrettable but inevitable, till your government changes its policies. I bear no personal animosity, Lieutenant Dominic Flandry. I far prefer friendship, and hope a measure of it may take root between us while we are together.

"As for your question, *datholch* is a civilian rather than a military rank." He did not speak in exact equivalents, for Merseia separated "civilian" and "military" differently from Terra, and less clearly; but Flandry got the idea. "It designates an aristocrat who heads an enterprise concerned with expanding the Race's frontier." (Frontier of knowledge, trade, influence, territory, or what? He didn't say, and quite likely it didn't occur to him that there was any distinction.) "As for my standing, I belong to the Vach Urdiolch and"—he stood up and touched his brow while he finished—"it is my high honor that a brother of my late noble father is, in the glory of the God, Almighty Roidhun of Merseia, the Race, and all holdings, dominions, and subordinates of the Race."

Flandry scrambled to his feet and yanked Djana to hers. "Salute!" he hissed in her ear, in Anglic. "Like me! This chap's a nephew of their grand panjandrum!"

Who might or might not be a figurehead, depending on the circumstances of his reign—and surely, that he was always elected from among the Urdiolchs, by the Hands of the Vachs and the heads of Merseian states organized otherwise than the anciently dominant culture—from among the Urdiolchs, the only landless Vach—surely this was in part a check on his powers—but surely, too, the harshest, most dictatorial Protector regarded his Roidhun with something of the same awe and pride that inspired the lowliest "foot" or "tail"—for the Roidhun stood for the God, the unity, and the hope of a warrior people—Flandry's mind swirled close to chaos before he brought it under control.

"Be at ease." Ydwyr reseated himself and gestured the humans to do likewise. "I myself am nothing but a scientist." He leaned forward. "Of course, I served my time in the Navy, and continue to hold a reserve commission; but my interests are xenological. This is essentially a research station. Talwin was discovered by accident about—uh-h-h-h —fifteen Terran years ago. Astronomers had noted an unusual type of pulsar in this vicinity: extremely old, close to extinction. A team of physicists went for a look. On the way back, taking routine observations as they traveled, they detected the unique orbital scramble around Siekh and investigated it too."

Flandry thought sadly that humans might well have visited that pulsar in early days—it was undoubtedly noted in the pilot's data for these parts, rare objects being navigationally useful—but that none of his folk in the present era would venture almost to the ramparts of a hostile realm just to satisfy their curiosity.

Ydwyr was proceeding: "When I learned about Talwin's extraordinary natives, I decided they must be studied, however awkwardly near your borders this star lies."

Flandry could imagine the disputes and wire-pullings that had gone on, and the compromise which finally was reached, that Talwin should also be an advanced base for keeping an eye on the Terrans. No large cost was involved, nor any large risk . . . nor any large chance of glory and promotion, which last fact helped explain Morioch's eagerness to wring his prisoners dry.

The lieutenant wet his lips. "You, uh, you are most kind, sir," he said; the honorific appeared implicitly in the pronoun. "What do you wish of us?"

"I would like to get to know you well," Ydwyr said frankly. "I have studied your race in some detail; I have met individual members of it; I have assisted in diplomatic business; but you remain almost an abstraction, almost a complicated forcefield rather than a set of beings with minds and desires and souls. It is curious, and annoying, that I should be better acquainted with Domrath and Ruadrath than with Terrans, our one-time saviors and teachers, now our mighty rivals. I want to converse with you.

"Furthermore, since any intelligence agent must know considerable xenology, you may be able to help us in our research on the autochthons here. Of a different species and culture, you may gain insights that have escaped us.

"This is the more true, and you are the more intriguing in your own right, because of who you are. By virtue of my family connections, I obtained the story—or part of the story—behind the Starkad affair. You are either very capable, Dominic Flandry, or else very lucky, and I wonder if there may not be a destiny in you."

82

The term he used was obscure, probably archaic, and the man had to guess its meaning from context and cognation. Fate? Mana? Odd phrasing for a scientist.

"In return," Ydwyr finished, "I will do what I can to protect you." With the bleak honesty of his class: "I do not promise to succeed."

"Do you think, sir . . . I might ever be released?" Flandry asked.

"No. Not with the information you hold. Or not without so deep a memory wiping that no real personality would remain. But you should find life tolerable in my service."

If you find my service worthwhile, Flandry realized, *and if higher-ups don't overrule you when they learn about me.* "I have no doubt I shall, sir. Uh, maybe I can begin with a suggestion, for you to pass on to the *qanryf* if you see fit."

Ydwyr waited.

"I heard the lords speaking about, uh, ordering that the man who hired me—Leon Ammon—" *might as well give him the name, it'll be in Rax's dispatch* "—that he be eliminated, to eliminate knowledge of Wayland from the last Terrans. I'd suggest going slow and cautious there. You know how alarmed and alerted they must be, sir, even on sleepy old Irumclaw Base, when I haven't reported in. It'd be risky passing on an order to your agents, let alone having them act. Best wait awhile. Besides, I don't know myself how many others Ammon told. I should think your operatives ought to make certain they've identified everyone who may be in on the secret, before striking.

"And there's no hurry, sir. Ammon hasn't any ship of his own, nor dare he hire one of the few civilian craft around. Look how easy it was to subvert the interplanetary ferrier we used, without ever telling him what a treasure was at stake. Oh, you haven't heard that detail yet, have you, sir? It's part of how I was trapped.

"Ammon will have to try discovering what went wrong; then killing those who betrayed him, or those he can find or thinks he's found; and making sure they don't kill him first; and locating another likely-looking scoutship pilot, and sounding him out over months, and waiting for assignment rotation to put him on the route passing nearest Wayland, and— Well, don't you see, sir, nothing's going to happen that you need bother about for more than a year? If you want to be ultra-cautious, I suppose you can post a warcraft in the Mimirian System; I can tell you the coordinates, though frankly, I think you'd be wasting your

83

effort. But mainly, sir, your side has everything to lose and nothing to gain by moving fast against Ammon."

"*Khraich.*" Ydwyr rubbed palm across chin, a sandpapery sound—under the storm-noise—despite his lack of beard. "Your points are well taken. Yes, I believe I will recommend that course to Morioch. And, while my authority in naval affairs is theoretically beneath his, in practice—"

His glance turned keen. "I take for granted, Dominic Flandry, you speak less in the hope of ingratiating yourself with me than in the hope of keeping events on Irumclaw in abeyance until you can escape."

"Uh—uh, well, sir—"

Ydwyr chuckled. "Don't answer. I too was a young male, once. I do trust you won't be so foolish as to try a break. If you accomplished it, the planet would soon kill you. If you failed, I would have no choice but to turn you over to Morioch's inquisitors."

CHAPTER
XIII

The airbus was sturdier and more powerful than most, to withstand violent weather. But the sky simmered quiet beneath its high gray cloud deck when Flandry went to the Domrath.

That was several of Talwin's eighteen-hour days after he had arrived. Ydwyr had assigned the humans a room in the building that housed his scientific team. They shared the mess there. The Merseian civilians were cordial and interested in them. The two species ate each other's food and drank each other's ale with, usually, enjoyment as well as nutrition. Flandry spent the bulk of his time getting back into physical shape and oriented about this planet. Reasonably reconciled with Djana—who'd been caught in the fortunes of war, he thought, and who now did everything she could to mollify her solitary fellow human—he made his nights remarkably pleasant. In general, aside from being a captive whose fate was uncertain and from having run out of tobacco, he found his stay diverting.

Nor was she badly off. She had little to fear, perhaps much to gain. If she never returned to the Empire, well, that was no particular loss when other humans lived under the Roidhunate. Like a cat that has landed on its feet, she set about studying her new environment. This involved long conversations with the thirty-plus members of Ydwyr's group. She had no Merseian language except for the standard loan words, and none of her hosts had more than the sketchiest Anglic. But they kept a translating computer for use with the natives. The memory bank of such a device regularly included the major tongues of known space.

She'll make out, Flandry decided. *Her kind always does, right up to the hour of the asp.*

Then Ydwyr offered him a chance to accompany a party bound for Seething Springs. He jumped at it, both from curiosity and from pragmatism. If he was to be a quasi-slave, he might have a worse master; he must therefore see about pleasing the better one. Moreover, he had not inwardly surrendered hope of gaining his freedom, to which end anything he learned might prove useful.

Half a dozen Merseians were in the expedition. "It's fairly ordinary procedure, but should be stimulating," said Cnif hu Vanden, xenophysiologist, who had gotten friendliest with him. "The Domrath are staging their fall move to hibernating grounds—in the case of this particular group, from Seething Springs to Mt. Thunderbelow. We've never observed it among them, and they do have summertime customs that don't occur elsewhere, so maybe their migration has special features too." He gusted a sigh. "This pouchful of us . . . to fathom an entire world!"

"I know," Flandry answered. "I've heard my own scholarly acquaintances groan about getting funds." He spread his hands. "Well, what do you expect? As you say: an entire world. It took our races till practically yesterday to begin to understand their home planets. And now, when we have I don't know how many to walk on if we know the way—"

Cnif was typical of the problem, crossed his mind. The stout, yellowish, slightly flat-faced male belonged to no Vach; his ancestors before unification had lived in the southern hemisphere of Merseia, in the Republic of Lafdigu, and to this day their descendants maintained peculiarities of dress and custom, their old language and many of their old laws. But Cnif was born in a colony; he had not seen the mother world until he came there for advanced education, and many of its ways were strange to him.

The bus glided forward. The first valve of the hangar heatlock closed behind it, the second opened, and it climbed with a purr of motor and whistle of wind. At 5000 meters it leveled off and bore north-northeast. That course by and large followed the river. Mainly the passengers sat mute, preparing their kits or thinking their thoughts. Merseians never chattered like humans. But Cnif pointed out landmarks through the windows.

"See, behind us, at the estuary, what we call Barrier Bay. In early winter it becomes choked with icebergs and floes, left by the receding waters. When they melt in spring, the turbulence and flooding is unbelievable."

The stream wound like a somnolent snake through the myriad blues of jungle. "We call it the Golden River in spite of its being silt-brown. Auriferous sands, you see, washed down from the mountains. Most of the place names are unavoidably ours. Some are crude translations from Domrath terms. The Ruadrath don't have place

86

names in our sense, which is why we seldom borrow from them."

Cnif's words for the aborigines were artificial. They had to be. "Dom" did represent an attempt at pronouncing what one of the first communities encountered called themselves; but "-rath" was an Eriau root meaning, approximately, "folk," and "Ruadrath" had originally referred to a class of nocturnal supernatural beings in a Merseian mythology—"elves."

The forested plain gave way to ever steeper foothills. The shadowless gray light made contours hard to judge, but Flandry could see how the Golden ran here through a series of deep canyons. "Those are full to the brim when the glaciers melt," Cnif said. "But we've since had so much evaporation that the level is well down; and we'll soon stop getting rain, it'll become first fog, later snow and hail. We are at the end of summer."

Flandry reviewed what he had read and heard at the base. Talwin went about Siekh in an eccentric ellipse which, of course, had the sun at one focus. You could define summer arbitrarily as follows: Draw a line through that focus, normal to the major axis, intersecting the curve at two points. Then summer was the six-month period during which Talwin passed from one of those points, through periastron, to the other end of the line segment. Fall was the six weeks or so which it took to get from the latter point to the nearest intersection of the minor axis with the ellipse. Winter occupied the fifteen months wherein Talwin swung out to its remotest distance and back again to the opposite minor-axis intersection. Thereafter spring took another six weeks, until the point was reached again which defined the beginning of summer.

In practice, things were nowhere near that simple. There were three degrees of axial tilt; there were climatic zones; there were topographical variations; above all, there was the thermal inertia of soil, rock, air, and water. Seasons lagged planetary positions by an amount depending on where you were and on any number of other factors, not every one of which the Merseians had unraveled.

Nonetheless, once weather started to change, it changed with astonishing speed. Cnif had spoken in practical rather then theoretical terms.

Vague through haze, the awesome peaks of the Hellkettle Mountains came to view beyond their foothills. Several plumes of smoke drifted into gloomy heaven. An isolated titan stood closer, lifting scarred black flanks in cliffs and talus slopes and grotesquely congealed lava beds, up to a cone that was quiet now but only for now. "Mt. Thunder-below." The bus banked left and descended on a long slant, above a tributary of the Golden. Vapors roiled white on those waters. "The Neverfreeze River. Almost all streams, even the biggest, go stiff in winter; but this is fed by hot springs, that draw their energy from the volcanic depths. That's why the Ruadrath—of Wirrda's, I mean—have prospered so well in these parts. Aquatic life remains active and furnishes a large part of their food."

Fuming rapids dashed off a plateau. In the distance, forest gave way to sulfur beds, geysers, and steaming pools. The bus halted near the plateau edge. Flandry spied a clearing and what appeared to be a village, though seeing was poor through the tall trees. While the bus hovered, the expedition chief spoke through its outercom. "We've distributed miniature transceivers," Cnif explained to Flandry. "It's best to ask leave before landing. Not that we have anything to fear from them, but we don't want to make them shy. We lean backwards. Why . . . do you know, a few years past, a newcomer to our group blundered into a hibernation den before the males were awake. He thought they would be, but they weren't; that was an especially cold spring. Two of them were aroused. They tore him to shreds. And we refrained from punishment. They weren't really conscious; instinct was ruling them."

His tone—insofar as a human could interpret—was not unkindly but did imply: Poor animals, they aren't capable of behaving better. *You gatortails get a lot of dynamism out of taking for granted you're the natural future lords of the galaxy,* the man thought, *but your attitude has its disadvantages. Not that you deliberately antagonize any other races, provided they give you no trouble. But you don't use their talents as fully as you might. Ydwyr seems to understand this. He mentioned that I could be valuable as a non-Merseian—which suggests he'd like to have team members from among the Roidhunate's client species—but I imagine he had woes enough pushing his project through a reluctant government, without bucking attitudes so ingrained that the typical Merseian isn't even conscious of them.*

Given a radio link to the base, the expedition leader didn't bother with a vocalizer. He spoke Eriau directly to the computer back there. It rendered his phrases into the dialect spoken here at Ktha-g-klek, to the limited extent that the latter was "known" to its memory bank. Grunting, clicking noises emerged from the minisets of whatever beings listened in the village. The reverse process operated, via relay by the bus. An artificial Merseian voice said: "Be welcome. We are in a torrent of toil, but can happen a sharing of self is possible."

"The more if we can help you with your transportation," the leader offered.

The Dom hesitated. *A primitive's conservatism,* Flandry recognized. *He can't be sure airlifts aren't unlucky, or whatever.* Finally: "Come to us."

That was not quickly done. First everybody aboard must get into his heat suit. One had been modified for Flandry. It amounted to a white coverall bedecked with pockets and sheaths; boots; gauntlets—everything insulated around a web of thermoconductor strands. A fishbowl helmet was equipped with chowlock, mechanical wipers, two-way sonic amplification, and short-range radio. A heat pump, hooked to the thermoconductors and run off accumulators, was carried on a backpack frame. Though heavy, the rig was less awkward than might have been expected. Its weight was well distributed; the gloves were thick and stiff, but apparatus was designed with that in mind, and plectrum-like extensions could be slipped over the fingers for finer work. *Anyway,* Flandry thought, *consider the alternative.*

It's not that man or Merseian can't survive awhile in this sauna. I expect we could, if the while be fairly short. It's that we wouldn't particularly want to survive.

Checked out, the party set down its vehicle and stepped forth. At this altitude, relay to base continued automatically.

Flandry's first awareness was of weight, enclosure, chuttering pump, cooled dried air blown at his nostrils. Being otherwise unprocessed, the atmosphere bore odors—growth, decay, flower and animal exudations, volcanic fumes—that stirred obscure memories at the back of his brain. He dismissed them and concentrated on his surroundings.

The river boomed past a broad meadow, casting spray and steam over its banks. Above and on every side loomed the jungle. Trees grew high, brush grew wide, leaf crowding serrated blue leaf until the eye soon lost itself in dripping murk. But the stems looked frail, pulpy, and the leaves were drying out; they rattled against each other, the fallen ones scrittled before a breeze, the short life of summer's forest drew near to an end.

Sturdier on open ground was that vegetable family the Merseians called *wair:* as widespread, variegated, and ecologically fundamental as grass on Terra. In spring it grew

89

from a tough-hulled seed, rapidly building a cluster of foliage and a root that resembled a tuber without being one. The leaves of the dominant local species were ankle height and lacy. They too were withering, the wair was going dormant; but soon, in fall, it would consume its root and sprout seeds, and when frost cracked their pods, the seeds would fall to earth.

Darkling over treetops could be glimpsed Mt. Thunderbelow. A slight shudder went through Flandry's shins, he heard a rumble, the volcano had cleared its throat. Smoke puffed forth.

But the Domrath were coming. He focused on them.

Life on Talwin had followed the same general course as on most terrestroid planets. Differences existed. It would have been surprising were there none. Thus, while tissues were principally built of L-amino proteins in water solution like Flandry's or Cnif's, here they normally metabolized levo sugars. A man could live on native food, if he avoided the poisonous varieties; but he must take the dietary capsules the Merseians had prepared.

Still, the standard division into photosynthetic vegetable and oxygen-breathing animal had occurred, and the larger animals were structurally familiar with their interior skeletons, four limbs, paired eyes and ears. Set beside many sophonts, the Domrath would have looked homelike.

They were bipeds with four-fingered hands, their outline roughly anthropoid except for the proportionately longer legs and huge, clawed, thickly soled feet necessary to negotiate springtime swamps and summer hardpan. The skin was glabrous, bluish, with brown and black mottlings that were beginning to turn gaudy colors as mating season approached. The heads were faintly suggestive of elephants': round, with beady eyes, large erect ears that doubled as cooling surfaces, a short trunk that was a chemosensor and a floodtime snorkel, small down-curving tusks on the males. The people wore only loincloths, loosely woven straw cloaks to help keep off "insects," necklaces and other ornaments of bone, shell, horn, teeth, tinted clay. Some of their tools and weapons were bronze, some—incongruously—paleolithic.

That much was easily grasped. And while their size was considerable, adult males standing over two meters and massing a hundred or more kilos, females even larger, it was not overwhelming. They were bisexual and viviparous. Granted, they were not mammals. A mother fed her infants by regurgitation. Bodies were poikilothermic, though

90

now functioning at a higher rate than any Terran reptile. That was not unheard of either.

Nonetheless, Flandry thought, it marked the foundation of their uniqueness. For when your energy, your very intelligence was a function of temperature; when you not only slept at night, but spent two-thirds of your life among the ghostly half-dreams of hibernation—

About a score had come to meet the xenologists, with numerous young tagging after. The grownups walked in ponderous stateliness. But several had burdens strapped on their backs; and behind them Flandry saw others continue work, packing, loading bundles onto carrier poles, sweeping and garnishing soon-to-be-deserted houses.

The greeting committee stopped a few meters off. Its leader elevated his trunk while dipping his ax. Sounds that a human palate could not reproduce came from his mouth. Flandry heard the computer's voice in his radio unit. "Here is Seething Springs. I am"—no translation available, but the name sounded like "G'ung"—"who speaks this year for our tribe." An intonation noted, in effect, that "tribe" (Eriau *maddeuth,* itself not too close an equivalent of the Anglic word by which Flandry rendered it) was a debatable interpretation of the sound G'ung made, but must serve until further studies had deepened comprehension of his society. "Why have you come?"

The question was not hostile, nor was the omission of a spoken welcome. The Domrath were gregarious, unwarlike although valiant fighters at need, accustomed to organizing themselves in nomadic bands. And, while omnivorous, they didn't make hunting a major occupation. Their near ancestors had doubtless lived entirely off the superabundant plant life of summer. Accordingly, they had no special territorial instincts. Except for their winter dens, it did not occur to them that anyone might not have a perfect right to be anywhere.

The Seething Springs folk were unusual in returning annually to permanent buildings, instead of constructing temporary shelters wherever they chanced to be. And this custom had grown up among them only because their hibernation site was not too far from this village. No one had challenged their occupation of it.

Quite simply and amiably, G'ung wondered what had brought the Merseians.

"We explained our reasons when last we visited you . . . with gifts," their leader reminded. His colleagues bore trade goods, metal tools and the like, which had hitherto delighted all recipients. "We wish to learn about your tribe."

"Is understood." Neither G'ung nor his group acted wildly enthusiastic.

No Domrath had shown fear of the Merseians. Being formidable animals, they had never developed either timidity or undue aggressiveness; being at an early prescientific stage, they lived among too many marvels and mysteries to see anything terrifyingly strange about spaceships bearing extraplanetarians; and Ydwyr had enforced strict correctness in every dealing with them. So why did these hesitate?

The answer was manifest as G'ung continued: "But you came before in high summer. Fastbreaking Festival was past, the tribes had dispersed, food was ample and wit was keen. Now we labor to bring the season's gatherings to our hibernation place. When we are there, we shall feast and mate until we drowse off. We have no time or desire for sharing self with outsiders."

"Is understood, G'ung," the Merseian said. "We do not wish to hamper or interfere. We do wish to observe. Other tribes have we watched as fall drew nigh, but not yours, and we know your ways differ from the lowlanders' in more than one regard. For this privilege we bid gifts and, can happen, the help of our flying house to transport your stores."

The Domrath snorted among themselves. They must be tempted but unsure. Against assistance in the hard job of moving stuff up toward Mt. Thunderbelow must be balanced a change in immemorial practice, a possible angering of gods . . . yes, it was known the Domrath were a religious race. . . .

"Your words shall be shared and chewed on," G'ung decided. "We shall assemble tonight. Meanwhile is much to do while light remains." The darkness of Talwin's clouded summer was pitchy; and in this dry period, fires were restricted and torches tabooed. He issued no spoken invitation, that not being the custom of his folk, but headed back. The Merseians followed with Flandry.

The village was carefully laid out in a spiderweb pattern of streets—for defense? Buildings varied in size and function, from hut to storage shed, but were all of stone, beautifully dressed, dry-laid, and chinked. Massive wooden beams supported steeply pitched sod roofs. Both workmanship and dimensions—low ceilings, narrow doorways, slit windows with heavy shutters—showed that, while the Domrath used this place, they had not erected it.

They boiled about, a hundred or so of every age; doubtless more were on the trail to the dens. Voices and footfalls surged around. In spite of obvious curiosity, no one halted work above a minute to stare at the visitors. Autumn was too close.

At a central plaza, where the old cooked a communal meal over a firepit, G'ung showed the Merseians some benches. "I will speak among the people," he said. "Come day's end, you shall receive us here and we shall share self on the matter you broach. Tell me first: would the Ruadrath hold with your plan?"

"I assure you the Ruadrath have nothing against it," Cnif said.

From what I've studied, Flandry thought, *I'm not quite sure that's true, once they find out.*

"I have glimpsed a Ruad—I think—when I was small and spring came early," said an aged female. "That you see them each year—" She wandered off, shaking her head.

With Cnif's assent, Flandry peeked into a house fronting on the square. He saw a clay floor, a hearth and smokehole, daises along two sides with shelves above. Bright unhuman patterns glowed on walls and intricately carved timbers. In one corner stood a loaded rack, ready to go. But from the rafters, with ingenious guards against animals, hung dried fruits and cured meat—though the Domrath were rarely eaters of flesh. A male sat carefully cleaning and greasing bronze utensils, knives, bowls, an ax, a saw. His female directed her young in tidying the single room while she spread the daises with new straw mats.

Flandry greeted the family. "Is this to be left?" he asked. It seemed like quite a bit for these impoverished savages.

"In rightness, what else?" the male replied. He didn't stop his work, nor appear to notice that Flandry was not a Merseian. In his eyes, the differences were probably negligible. "The metal is of the Ruadrath, as is the house. For use we give payment, that they may be well pleased with us when they come out of the sea." He did pause then, to make a sign that might be avertive or might be reverent —or both or neither, but surely reflected the universal sense of a mortal creature confronting the unknown. "Such is the law, by which our forebears lived while others died. *Thch ra'a.*"

Ruadrath: elves, gods, winter ghosts.

CHAPTER
XIV

More and more, as the weeks of Flandry's absence passed, her existence took on for Djana an unreality. Or was it that she began slowly to enter a higher truth, which muted the winds outside and made the walls around her shadowy?

Not that she thought about it in that way, save perhaps when the magician wove her into a spell. Otherwise she lived in everydayness. She woke in the chamber that the man had shared with her. She exercised and groomed herself out of habit, because her living had hitherto depended on her body. At mess she stood respectfully aside while the Merseians went through brief rituals religious, familial, and patriotic—oddly impressive and stirring, those big forms and deep voices, drawn steel and talking drums— and afterward joined in coarse bread, raw vegetables, *gwydh*-milk cheese, and the Terran-descended tea which they raised throughout the Roidhunate. There followed study, talk, sometimes a special interview, sometimes recreation for a while; a simple lunch; a nap in deference to her human circadian rhythm; more study, until evening's meat and ale. (Since Merseia rotated at about half the rate of Talwin, a night had already gone over the land.) Later she might have further conversation, or attend a concert or recorded show or amateur performance of something traditional; or she might retire alone with a tape. In any event, she was early abed.

Talk, like perusal of a textreel or watching of a projection, was via the linguistic computer. It had plenty of spare channels, and could throw out a visual translation as easily as a sonic one. However, she was methodically being given a working knowledge of Eriau, along with an introduction to Merseian history and culture.

She cooperated willingly. Final disposition of her case lay with superiors who had not yet been heard from. At worst, though, she wasn't likely to suffer harm—given a prince of the blood on her side—and at best . . . well, who dared predict? Anyway, her education gave her something to do. And as it advanced, it started interesting, at last entrancing her.

Merseia, rival, aggressor, troublemaker, menace lairing out beyond Betelgeuse: she'd accepted the slogans like everybody else, never stopping to think about them. Oh, yes, the Merseians were terrible, but they lived far off and the Navy was supposed to keep them there while the diplomatic corps maintained an uneasy peace, and she had troubles of her own.

Here she dwelt among beings who treated her with gruff kindness. Once you got to know them, she thought, they were . . . they had homes and kin the same as people, that they missed the same as people; they had arts, melodies, sports, games, jokes, minor vices, though of course you had to learn their conventions, their whole style of thinking, before you could appreciate it. . . . They didn't want war with Terra, they only saw the Empire as a bloated sick monstrosity which had long outlived its usefulness but with senile cunning contrived to hinder and threaten *them*. . . . No, they did not dream of conquering the galaxy, that was absurd on the face of it, they simply wanted freedom to range and rule without bound, and "rule" did not mean tyranny over others, it meant just that others should not stand in the way of the full outfolding of that spirit which lay in the Race. . . .

A spirit often hard and harsh, perhaps, but bone-honest with itself; possessed of an astringency that was like a sea breeze after the psychic stench of what Djana had known; not jaded or rootless, but reaching for infinity and for a God beyond infinity, while planted deep in the consciousness of kinship, heroic ancestral memories, symbols of courage, pride, sacrifice. . . . Djana felt it betokened much that the chief of a Vach—not quite a clan—was called not its Head but its Hand.

Were those humans who served Merseia really traitors . . . to anything worth their loyalty?

But it was not this slow wondering that made the solid world recede from her. It was Ydwyr the Seeker and his spells; and belike they had first roused the questions in her.

To start with, he too had merely talked. His interest in her background, experiences, habits, and attitudes appeared strictly scientific. As a rule they met *à deux* in his office. "Thus I need not be a nephew of the Roidhun," he explained wryly. Fear stabbed her for a second. He gave her a shrewd regard and added, "No one is monitoring our translator channel."

She gathered nerve to say, "The *qanryf*—"

"We have had our differences," Ydwyr replied, "but Morioch is a male of honor."

She thought: *How many Imperial officers in this kind of setup would dare skip precautions against snooping and blackmail?*

He had a human-type chair built for her, and poured her a glass of arthberry wine at each colloquy. Before long she was looking forward to the sessions and wishing he were less busy elsewhere, coordinating his workers in the field and the data they brought back. He didn't press her for answers, he relaxed and let conversation ramble and opened for her the hoard of his reminiscences about adventures on distant planets.

She gathered that xenology had always fascinated him and that he was seldom home. Almost absent-mindedly, in obligation to his Vach, he had married and begotten; but he took his sons with him from the time they were old enough to leave the gynaeceum until they were ready for their Navy hitches. Yet he did not lack warmth. His subordinates adored him. When he chanced to speak of the estate where he was born and raised, his parents and siblings, the staff whose fathers had served his fathers for generations, she came to recognize tenderness.

Then finally—it was dark outside, the hot still dark of summer's end, heat lightning aflicker beyond stockade and skeletal trees—he summoned her; but when she entered the office, he rose and said: "Let us go to my private quarters."

For a space she was again frightened. He bulked so big, so gaunt and impassive in his gray robe, and they were so alone together. A fluoro glowed cold, and the air that slid and whispered across her skin had likewise gone chill.

He smiled his Merseian smile, which she had learned to read as amicable. Crinkles radiated through the tiny scales of his skin, from eyes and mouth. "I want to show you something I keep from most of my fellows," he said. "You might understand where they cannot."

The little voicebox hung around his neck, like the one around hers, spoke with the computer's flat Anglic. She filled that out with his Eriau. No longer did the language sound rough and guttural; it was, in truth, rather soft, and rich in tones. She could pick out individual words by now. She heard nothing in his invitation except—

—*the father I never knew.*

Abruptly she despised herself for what she had feared. How must she look to him? Face: hag-thin, wax-white,

96

save for the bizarrely thick and red lips; behind it, two twisted flaps of cartilage. Body: dwarfish, scrawny, bulge-breasted, pinch-waisted, fat-bottomed, tailless, feet outright deformed. Skin: no intricate pattern of delicate flexible overlap; a rubberiness relieved only by lines and coarse pores; and hair, everywhere hair in ridiculous bunches and tufts, like fungus on a corpse. Odor: what? Sour? Whatever it was, no lure for a natural taste.

Men! she thought. *God, I don't mean to condemn Your work, but You also made the dogs men keep, and don't You agree they're alike, those two breeds? Dirty, smelly, noisy, lazy, thievish, quick to attack when you aren't watching, quick to run or cringe when you are; they're useless, they create nothing, you have to wait on them, listen to their boastful bayings, prop up their silly little egos till they're ready to slobber over you again. . . .*

I'm sorry. Jesus wore the shape of a man, didn't he?

But he wore it—in pity—because we needed him—and what've we done with his gift?

Before her flashed the image of a Merseian Christ, armed and shining, neither compassionate nor cruel but the Messiah of a new day. . . . She hadn't heard of any such belief among them. Maybe they had no need of redemption; maybe they were God's chosen. . . .

Ydwyr caught her hands between his, which were cool and dry. "Djana, are you well?"

She shook the dizziness from her head. *Too much being shut in. Too much soaking myself in a world that can't be mine. Nicky's been gone too long. (I saw a greyhound once, well-trained, proud, clean and swift. Nicky's a greyhound.) I can't get away from my humanness. And I shouldn't want to, should I?* "N-nothing, sir. I felt a little faint. I'll be all right."

"Come rest." Stooping, he took her arm—a Terran gesture she had told him about—and led her through the inner curtain to his apartment.

The first room was what she might have expected and what officers of the base had no doubt frequently seen: emblem of the Vach Urdiolch, animation of a homeworld scene where forested hills plunged toward an ocean turbulent beneath four moons, shelves of books and mementos, racked weapons, darkly shimmering drapes; on the resilient floor, a carved and inlaid table of black wood, a stone in a shallow crystal bowl of water, an alcove shrine, and nothing else except spaciousness. One archway, half unscreened, gave on a monastic bedchamber and 'fresher cubicle.

But they passed another hanging. She stopped in the dusk beyond and exclaimed.

"Be seated if you wish." He helped her shortness to the top of a couch upholstered in reptilian hide. The locks swirled over her shoulders as she stared about.

The mounted skulls of two animals, one horned, one fanged; convoluted tubes and flasks crowding a bench in the gloom of one corner; a monolith carved with shapes her eye could not wholly follow, that must have required a gravsled to move; a long-beaked leathery-skinned thing, the span of its ragged wings equal to her height, that sat unblinking on its gnarled perch; and more and more, barely lit by flambeaux in curiously wrought sconces, whose restless blue glow made shadows move like demons, whose crackling was a thin song that almost meant something she had forgotten, whose smoke was pungent and soon tingled in her brain.

She looked up to the craggy highlights of Ydwyr's countenance, tremendously above her. "Do not be afraid," said the lion voice. "These are not instruments of the darkness, they are pathfinders to enter it."

He sat down on his tail, bringing his ridged head level with hers. Reflections moved like flames deep within the caverns under his brow ridges. But his speech stayed gentle, even wistful.

"The Vach Urdiolch are the landless ones. So is the Law, that they may have time and impartiality to serve the Race. Our homes, where we have dwelt for centuries, we keep by leasehold. Our wealth comes less from ancient dues than from what we may win offplanet. This has put us in the forefront of the Race's outwardness; but it has also brought us closest to the unknowns of worlds never ours.

"A witch was my nurse. She had served us since my grandfather was a cub. She had four arms and six legs, what was her face grew between her upper shoulders, she sang to me in tones I could not always hear, and she practiced magic from the remembered Ebon Mountains of her home. Withal, she was good and faithful; and in me she found a ready listener.

"I think that may be what turned me toward searching out the ways of alien folk. It helps Merseia, yes; we need to know them; but I have wanted their lore for its own sake. And Djana, I have not perpetually found mere primitive superstition. A herb, a practice, a story, a philosophy . . . how dare we say nothing real is in them, when we come new to a world that gave birth to those who live on it? Among folk who had no machines I saw, a few times, happenings that I do not believe any machine could bring about.

"In a sense, I became a mystic; in another sense, none, for where is the border between 'natural' and 'transcendental'? Hypnosis, hysterical strength and stigmata, sensory heightening, psychosomatics, telepathy—such things are scorned in the scientific youth of civilizations, later accepted, when understanding has grown. I am simply using techniques that may, perhaps, advance comprehension where gauges and meters cannot.

"Once I got leave to visit Chereion. That is the most eldritch planet I have seen, a dominion of the Roidhunate but only, I think, because that serves the ends of its dwellers, whatever those ends are. For they are old, old. They had a civilization a million years ago that may have reached beyond this galaxy, where we have barely started to burrow about at the end of one spiral arm. It disappeared; they cannot or will not say why, and it suits a few of them to be too useful to Merseia for us to risk angering the rest. Yes, we haughty conquerors walk softly among them!

"I was received among the disciples of Aycharaych, in his castle at Raal. He has looked deeper into the mind—not the mind of his people, or yours, or any single one, but somehow into that quality of pandemic Mind which the scientists deny can exist—he has looked deeper into this, I believe, than any other being alive. He could not evoke in me what I did not have to be evoked; or else he did not choose to. But he taught me what he said I could use; and without that skill, that way of existing in the cosmos, I would never have done half what I have. Think: in a single decade, we are well on the way to full communication with both races on Talwin.

"I want, not to probe your soul, Djana, but to join with you in exploring it. I want to know the inwardness of being human; and you may see what it is to be Merseian."

The flames danced and whispered among moving shadows; the figures on the monolith traced a path that could almost be followed; the smoke whirled in her veins; around her and through her crooned the lullaby voice of Father.

"Do not be afraid of what you see, Djana. These things are archaic, yes, they speak of pagan cults and witchcraft, but that is because they come from primeval sources, from the beast that lived before mind was kindled in it. One day these tokens may no longer be needed. Or perhaps they will be, perhaps they go deeper even than I imagine. I do not know and I want to know. It will help to mesh awarenesses with a human, Djana . . . no terrified captive, no lickspittle turncoat, no sniveler about peace and brotherhood, no pseudomorph grown up among us apart from his own breed . . . but one who has come to me freely, out of the depths of the commonalty that bred her, one who has known alike the glory and the tragedy of being human.

"These are symbols, Djana, certain objects, certain rites, which different thinking species have found will help raise buried parts of the soul. And brought forth, those parts can be understood, controlled, strengthened. Remember what the discipline of the body can do. Remember likewise the discipline of the spirit; calm, courage, capability can be learned, if the means are known; they take nothing but determination. Now ask yourself: What more remains?

"Djana, you could become *strong*."

"Yes," she said.

And she was gazing into the water, and the fire, and the crystal, and the shadows within. . . .

A hostel at night. Fire leaping red and gold, chuckling as it lights the comradely company, rough-hewn furniture, fiddler on a chair tuning to play a dance; at the table's far end, a woman, long-gowned, deep-bosomed, who bears a sheaf and an infant on her lap.

Wind. A black bird sudden athwart the pane. The sound of its beak rapping.

Descent down endless stairs in the dark, led by one who never looks back. The boat. The river.

On the far side they have no faces.

"I am sorry," Ydwyr said. "We do not keep a pharmacopoeia for your species. You must forgo drugs. Furthermore, the Old Way is not for you to tread to its end—nor me, I confess. We have the real world to cope with, and we will not do so by abandonment of reason.

"Tell me your dreams. If they grow too bad, call me on my private line—thus—and I will come to you, no matter the hour."

The snake that engirdles the universe lifts its starry head. It gapes. Scream. Run.

The coils hiss after. The swamp clings to feet. A million

100

years, a step a year out of the sucking muck, and the snake draws close behind.

Lightning. Sinking. Black waters.

He held her, simply held her, at night in her room. "From my viewpoint," he said, "I am gaining matchless experience with human archetypes." The dry practicality, itself comforting, yielded to mildness. A big hand stroked her hair. "But you, Djana, are more than a thing. You are becoming like a child to me, did you know? I want to raise you up again and lead you through this valley of shadows you must pass before you can stand by your own strength."

At mornwatch he left her. She slept a short while, but got to breakfast and subsequently continued her regular schooling. It did not keep her from dwelling within her dreams.

Outside, the first mists of autumn sneaked white over the wet earth.

The waters are peace. Dream, drowse . . . no, the snake is not dead.

The snake is not dead.

His poisonous teeth. Struggle. Scream. The warm waters are gone, drained out with a huge hollow roaring. Hollow, hollow.

The hollow sound of hoofs, shaking a bridge that nine dead kings could not make thunder. Light.

The snake burns backward from the light.

Raise hands to it. But bow down from its brilliance.

That blaze is off the spear of the Messiah.

"*Khraich.* I would be interested to know if an abortion was attempted on you. Not important, since you survived. Your need is to learn that you did survive, and that you can.

"Do you feel ready for another session this evening? I would like for you to come and concentrate on the Graven Stone. It seems to have traits in common with what I have read your Terran usage calls a . . . a mandala?"

A mirror.

The face within.

One comes from behind on soundless feet and holds a mirror to the mirror.

Endlessness dwindles toward nothingness.

At the heart of nothingness, a white spark. It flames,

and nothingness recoils and flees back outward to endlessness, while trumpets triumph.

"Ur-r-rh." Ydwyr scowled at her test scores. They sat prosaically in his living room—though what was prosaic about its austere serenity? "Something developing, beyond question. A hitherto unrealized potential—not telepathy. I'd hoped—"

"The Old Way to the One," she said, and watched the wall dissolve.

He gave her a long stare before he replied, crisply: "You have gone as far down that road as I dare take you, my dear. Perhaps not far enough, but I am not able—I suspect none less than Aycharaych would be able—to guide you further; and alone, you would lose yourself in yourself."

"Hm?" she said vaguely. "Ydwyr, I know I touched your mind, I felt you."

"Delusion. Mysticism is a set of symbols. Symbols are to live by, yes—why else banners?—but they are not to be confused with the reality for which they stand. While we know less about telepathy than psychologists usually pretend, we do know it's a perfectly physical phenomenon. Extremely long waves travel at light speed, subject to inverse-square diminution and the other laws of nature; the principles of encoding apply; nothing but the radical variation of sensitivity, from time to time and individual to individual, ever made its existence doubtful. Today we can identify it when it occurs.

"Whatever happened in these last experiments of ours, you are not becoming a telepathic receiver. An influence of that general nature was present, true. The meters registered it, barely over threshold level. But analysis shows you were not calling the signs I dealt with above-random accuracy. Instead, I was not dealing them completely at random.

"Somehow, slightly, unconsciously, you were *influencing* me toward turning up the signs you guessed I would be turning up."

"I wanted to reach you," Djana mumbled.

Ydwyr said sternly: "I repeat, we have entered realms where I am not fit to conduct you. The dangers are too great—principally to you, possibly to me. At a later date, maybe, Aycharaych—for the present, we stop. You shall return to the flesh world, Djana. No more magic. Tomorrow we set you to gymnastics and flogging, exhausting, uninspiring work with Eriau. That should bring you back."

He on the throne: "For that they have sinned beyond redemption, the sin that may not be forgiven, which is to blaspheme against the Holy Spirit, no more are they My people.

"Behold, I cast them from Me; and I will raise against them a new people under a new sun; and their name shall be Strength.

"Open now the book of the seven thunders."

Talwin's short autumn was closing when the ship came from headquarters. That was not Merseia. No domain like the Roidhunate could be governed from a single planet, even had the Race been interested in trying. However, she did bear a direct word from the Protector.

She stood on the field, slim, sleek, a destroyer with guns whippet-wicked against the sky, making a pair of counterparts from Morioch's command that were likewise in port look outmoded and a little foolish. The captured Terran scoutboat hunched in a corner, pathetic.

Few trees showed above the stockade. Early frosts had split their flimsy trunks and brought them down, already to crumble back into the soil. The air was cool and moist. Mists coiled about Merseians working outdoors; but overhead heaven reached clear, deep blue, and what clouds there were shone dazzling white beneath Siekh.

Djana was not invited to the welcoming ceremonies, nor had she anticipated it. Ydwyr gave her a quick intercom call—"Have no fears, I am authorized to handle your case, as I requested in my dispatch"—and wasn't that wonderful of him? She went for a walk, a real tramp, kilometers along the bluffs above the Golden River and back through what had been enclosing jungle and was becoming open tundra, space, freedom, full lungs and taut muscles, for hour after hour until she turned home of her own desire.

I've changed, she thought. *I still don't know how much.* The weeks under Ydwyr's—tutelage?—were vague in her recollection, often difficult or impossible to separate from the dreams of that time. Later she had gradually regained herself. But it was no longer the same self. Old Djana was scarred, frightened, greedy with the greed that tries to fill inner emptiness, lonely with the loneliness that dares not love. New Djana was . . . well, she was trying to find out. She was someone who would go for a hike and stop to savor the scarlet of a late-blooming flower. She was someone who, in honest animal wise, hoped Nicky would soon finish with his expedition, and daydreamed

103

about something between him and her that would last, but did not feel she needed him or anybody to guard her from monsters.

Maybe none existed. Dangers, of course, but dangers can't do worse than kill you, and they said in the Vachs, "He cannot respect life who does not respect death." No, wait, she *had* met monsters, back in the Empire. Though she no longer quailed at the remembrance of them, she could see they must be crushed underfoot before they poisoned the good beings like Ydwyr and Nicky and Ulfangryf and Avalrik and, well, yes, all right, in his fashion, Morioch. . . .

Wind lulled, tossing her hair, caressing her skin, which wore less clothes than she would formerly have required on this kind of day. Occasionally she tried to call to her the winged creatures she saw, and twice she succeeded; a bright guest sat on her finger and seemed content, till she told it to continue toward its hibernation. To her, the use of her power felt like being a child again—she had been, briefly, once in a rare while—and wishing hard. Ydwyr guessed that it was a variety of projective telepathy and that its sporadic appearance in her species had given rise to legends about geases, curses, and allurements.

But I can't control it most of the time, and don't care that I can't. I don't want to be a superwoman. I'm happy just to be a woman—a full female, no matter what race— which is what Ydwyr made me.

How can I thank him?

The compound court was deserted when she entered it. Probably all personnel were fraternizing with the ship's crew. Dusk was falling, chill increased minute by minute, the wind grew louder and stars blinked forth. She hurried to her room.

The intercom was lit. She punched the replay. It said: "Report to the *datholch* in his office immediately on return," with the time a Merseian hour ago. That meant almost four of Terra's; they split their day decimally.

Her heart bumped. She operated the controls as she had done when the nightmares came. "Are you there, Ydwyr?"

"You hear me," said the reassuringly professorial voice he could adopt. By now she seldom needed the computer.

She sped down empty halls to him. Remotely, she heard hoarse lusty singing. When Merseians celebrated, they were apt to do so at full capacity. The curtain at his door fell behind her to cut off that sound.

She held fist to breast and breathed hard. He rose from

the desk where he had been working. "Come," he said. The gray robe flapped behind him.

When they were secret among the torches and skulls, he leaned down through twilight and breathed—each word stirred the hair around her ear—

"The ship brought unequivocal orders. You are safe. They do not care about you, provided you do not bring the Terrans the information you have. But Dominic Flandry has powerful enemies. Worse, his mentor Max Abrams does; and they suspect the younger knows secrets of the older. He is to go back in the destroyer. The probing will leave mere flesh, which will probably be disposed of."

"Oh, Nicky," she said, with a breaking within her.

He laid his great hands on her shoulders, locked eyes with eyes, and went on: "My strong recommendation having been overruled, my protest would be useless. Yet I respect him, and I believe you have affection for him yourself. This thing is not right, neither for him nor for Merseia. Have you learned to honor clean death?"

She straightened. The Eriau language made it natural to say, "Yes, Ydwyr, my father."

"You know your intercom has been connected to the linguistic computer, which on a different channel is in touch with the expedition he is on," he told her. "It keeps no records unless specifically instructed. Under guise of a personal message, the kind that commonly goes from here to those in the field, you can tell him what you like. You have thus exchanged words before, have you not? None of his companions know Anglic. He could wander away— 'lost'—and cold is a merciful executioner."

She said with his firmness: "Yes, sir."

Back in her room she lay for a time crying. But the thought that flew in and out was: *He's good. He wouldn't let them gouge the mind out of my Nicky. No Imperial Terran would care. But Ydwyr is like most of the Race. He has honor. He is good.*

CHAPTER

XV

The fog of autumn's end hid Mt. Thunderbelow and all the highlands in wet gray that drowned vision within meters. Flandry shivered and ran a hand through his hair, trying to brush the water out. When he stooped and touched the stony, streaming ground, it was faintly warm; now and then he felt a shudder in it and heard the volcano grumble.

His Merseian companions walked spectral before and behind him, on their way up the narrow trail. Most of them he could not see, and the Domrath they followed were quite lost in the mists ahead.

But he had witnessed the departure of the natives from camp and could visualize them plodding toward their sleep: the hardiest males, their speaker G'ung at the rear. That was a position of some danger, when late-waking summer or early-waking winter carnivores might suddenly pounce. (It wouldn't happen this year, given a tail of outworld observers armed with blasters and slugthrowers. However, the customs of uncounted millennia are not fast set aside.) The Domrath were at their most vulnerable, overburdened with their own weight, barely conscious in an energy-draining chill.

Flandry sympathized. To think that heatsuits were needed a month ago! Such a short time remained to the xenologists that it hadn't been worthwhile bringing along electric-grid clothes. Trying to take attention off his discomfort, he ran through what he had seen.

Migration—from Ktha-g-klek to the grounds beneath this footpath, a well-watered meadowland on the slopes of Thunderbelow, whose peak brooded enormous over it. Unloading of the food hoard gathered during summer. Weaving of rude huts.

That was the happy time of year. The weather was mild for Talwin. The demoniac energy promoted by the highest temperatures gave way to a pleasant idleness. Intelligence dropped too, but remained sufficient for routine tasks and even rituals. A certain amount of foraging went on, more or less *ad libitum*. For the main part, though, fall was one long orgy. The Domrath ate till they were practically globular and made love till well after every nubile female had been impregnated. Between times they sang, danced, japed, and loafed. They paid scant attention to their visitors.

But Talwin swung further from Siekh; the spilling rains got colder, as did the nights and then the days; cloud cover broke, revealing sun and stars before it re-formed on the ground; wair and trees withered off; grazing and browsing animals vanished into their own hibernations; at morning the puddles were sheeted over with ice, which crackled when you stepped on it; the rations dwindled away, but that made no difference, because appetite dropped as the people grew sluggish; finally they dragged themselves by groups to those dens whither the last were now bound.

And back to base for us, Flandry thought, *and Judas, but I'll be glad to warm myself with Djana again! Why hasn't she called me for this long, or answered my messages? They claim she's all right. She'd better be, or I'll explode.*

The trail debouched on a ledge beneath an overhang. Black in the dark basaltic rock gaped a cave mouth. Extinct fumaroles, blocked off at the rear by collapse during eruptions, were common hereabouts, reasonably well sheltered from possible lava flows, somewhat warmed by the mountain's molten core. Elsewhere, most Domrath moved south for the winter, to regions where the cold would get mortally intense. They could stand temperatures far below freezing—among other things, their body fluids became highly salty in fall, and transpiration during sleep increased that concentration—but in north country at high altitudes, without some protection, they died. The folk of Seething Springs took advantage of naturally heated dens.

Among the basic problems which life on Talwin must solve was: How could hibernators and estivators prevent carnivores active in the opposite part of the year from eating them? Different species solved it in different ways: by camouflage; by shells or spines or poisonous tissues; by tunneling deep, preferably under rock; by seeking areas where glaciers would cover them; by being so prolific that a percentage were bound to escape attention; and on and on. The Domrath, who were large and possessed weapons, lashed out in blind berserkergang if they were roused; winter animals tended to develop an instinct to leave them alone. They remained subject to a few predators, but against these they constructed shelters, or went troglodyte as here.

Shivering with hands in jacket pockets, breath puffing forth to join the mists, Flandry stood by while G'ung shepherded his males into the den. They moved somnambulistically. "I think we can go inside," murmured the Merseian nearest the Terran. "Best together, ready for trouble. We can't predict how they'll react, and when I asked earlier, they told me they never remember this period clearly."

"Avoid contact," advised another.

The scientists formed up with a precision learned in their military service. Flandry joined. They hadn't issued him weapons, though otherwise they had treated him pretty much as an equal; but he could duck inside their square if violence broke loose.

It didn't. The Domrath seemed wholly unaware of them.

This cave was small. Larger ones contained larger groups, each of which had entered in a body. The floor had been heaped beforehand with leaves, hay, and coarse-woven blankets. The air within was less bleak than outside—according to Wythan Scarcheek's thermometer. Slowly, grunting, rustling the damp material, the Domrath groped and burrowed into it. They lay close together, the stronger protecting the weaker.

G'ung stayed alone on his feet. Heavily he peered through the gloom; heavily he moved to close a gate installed in the mouth. It was a timber framework covered with hides and secured by a leather loop to a post.

"Ngugakathch," he mumbled like one who talks in his sleep. "Shoa t'kuhkeh." No translation came from the computer. It didn't have those words. A magical formula, a prayer, a wish, a noise? How many years before the meaning was revealed?

"Best get out," a Merseian, shadowy in mist and murk, whispered.

"No, we can undo the catch after they're unconscious," the leader said as softly. "And reclose it from the outside; the crack'll be wide enough to reach through. Watch this. Watch well. No one has found anything quite similar."

A camera lens gleamed.

They would sleep, those bulky friendly creatures—Flandry reflected—through more than a Terran year of ice age. No, not sleep; hibernate: comatose, barely alive, nursing the body's fuel as a man in illimitable darkness would nurse the single lamp he had. A sharp stimulus could trig-

108

ger wakefulness, by some chemical chain the Merseians had not traced; and the murderous rage that followed was a survival mechanism, to dispose of any threat and return to rest before too great a reserve was spent. Even undisturbed, they were not few who would never wake again.

The first who did were the pregnant females. They responded to the weak warmth of early spring, went out into the storms and floods of that season, joined forces and nourished themselves on what food could be gotten, free of competition from their tribesmates. Those were revived by higher temperatures, when the explosion of plant growth was well under way. They came forth gaunt and irritable, and did little but eat till they were fleshed out.

Then—at least in this part of the continent—tribes customarily met with tribes at appointed places. Fastbreaking Festival was held, a religious ceremony which also reinforced interpersonal relationships and gave opportunity for new ones.

Afterward the groups dispersed. Coastal dwellers sought the shorelands where rising sea level and melting ice created teeming marshes. Inlanders foraged and hunted in the jungles, whose day-by-day waxing could almost be seen. The infants were born.

Full summer brought the ripeness of wair roots and other vegetables, the fat maturity of land and water animals. And its heat called up the full strength and ingenuity of the Domrath. That was needful to them; now they must gather for fall. Females, held closer to home by their young than the males, became the primary transmitters of what culture there was.

Autumn: retirement toward the hibernation dens; rest, merrymaking, gorging, breeding.

Winter and the long sleep.

G'ung fumbled with the gate. Leaned against the wall nearby was a stone-headed spear. *How long have they lived this way, locked into this cycle?* Flandry mused. *Will they ever break free of it? And if they do, what next? It's amazing how far they've come under these handicaps. Strike off the manacles of Talwin's year . . . somehow . . . and, hm, it could turn out that the new dominators of this part of the galaxy will look a bit like old god Ganesh.*

His communicator, and the Merseians', said with Cnif hu Vanden's voice: "Dominic Flandry."

"Quiet!" breathed the leader.

"Uh, I'll go outside," the man proposed. He slipped by the creakily closing gate and stood alone on the ledge. Fog eddied and dripped. Darkness was moving in. The cold deepened.

"Switch over to local band, Cnif," he said, and did himself. His free hand clenched till the nails bit. "What is this?"

"A call for you from base." The xenophysiologist, who had been assigned to watch the bus while the rest accompanied the last Domrath, sounded puzzled. "From your female. I explained you were out and could call her back later, but she insisted the matter is urgent."

"What—?"

"You don't understand? I certainly don't. She lets weeks go by with never a word to you, and suddenly calls—speaking fair Eriau, too—and can't wait. That's what comes of your human sex-equality nonsense. Not that the sex of a non-Merseian concerns us. . . . Well, I said I'd try to switch you in. Shall I?"

"Yes, of course," Flandry said. "Thank you." He appreciated Cnif's thoughtfulness. They'd gotten moderately close on this often rugged trip, helping each other—on this often monotonous trip, when days of waiting for something noteworthy were beguiled by swapping yarns. You could do worse than pass your life among friends like Cnif and Djana—

A click, a faint crackling, and her utterance, unnaturally level: "Nicky?"

"Here, wishing I were there," he acknowledged, trying for lightness. But the volcano growled in stone and air.

"Don't show surprise," said the quick Anglic words. "This is terrible news."

"I'm alone," he answered. *How very alone.* Night gnawed at his vision.

"Nicky, darling, I have to say goodbye to you. Forever."

"What? You mean you—" He heard his speech at once loud and muffled in the clouds, hers tiny and as if infinitely removed.

"No. You. Listen. I may be interrupted any minute."

Even while she spoke, he wondered what had wrought the change in her. She should have been half incoherent, not giving him the bayonet-bare account she did. "You must have been told, the Merseian ship's arrived. They'll take you away for interrogation. You'll be a vegetable before they kill you. Your party's due back soon, isn't it? Escape first. Die decently, Nicky. Die free and yourself."

It was strange how detached he felt, and stranger still that he noticed it. Perhaps he hadn't yet realized the import. He had seen beings mortally wounded, gaping at their hurts without immediate comprehension that their lives were running out of them. "How do you know, Djana? How can you be sure?"

"Ydwyr— Wait. Someone coming. Ydwyr's people, no danger, but if somebody from the ship gets curious about — Hold on."

Silence, fog, night seeping over a land whose wetness had started to freeze. A few faint noises and a wan gleam of light slipped past the cave gate. The Domrath must be snuggling down, the Merseians making a final inspection by dimmed flashbeams before leaving. . . .

"It's all right, Nicky. I wished him to go past. I guess his intention to look into my room wasn't strong, if he had any, because he did go past."

"What?" Flandry asked in his daze.

"I've been . . . Ydwyr's been working with me. I've learned, I've developed a . . . a talent. I can wish a person, an animal, to do a thing, and when I'm lucky, it will. But never mind!" The stiffness was breaking in her; she sounded more like the girl he had known. "Ydwyr's the one who saved you, Nicky. He warned me and said I should warn you. Oh, hurry!"

"What'll become of you?" The man spoke automatically. His main desire was to keep her voice in the circuit, in the night.

"Ydwyr will take care of me. He's a—he's noble. The Merseians aren't bad, except a few. We want to save you from them. If only—you—" Her tone grew indistinct and uneven. "Get away, darling. Before too late. I want t-t-to remember you . . . like you were—God keep you!" she wailed, and snapped the connection.

He stood for a timeless time until, "What's wrong, Dominic?" Cnif asked.

"Uh, *khraich,* a complicated story." Flandry shook himself. Anger flared. *No! I'll not go meekly off to their brain machines. Nor will I quietly cut my throat, or slip into the hills and gently become an icicle.* A child underneath moaned terror of the devouring dark; but the surface mind had mastery. *If they want to close down me and my personal universe, by Judas but they'll pay for their fun!*

"Dominic, are you there?"

"Yes." Flandry's head had gone winter clear. He had but to call them, and ideas and pieces of information sprang forward. Not every card had been dealt. Damn near every one, agreed, and his two in this hand were a deuce and a four; but they were the same suit, which meant a straight flush remained conceivable in those spades which formerly were swords.

"Yes. I was considering what she told me, Cnif. That she's about decided to go over to the Roidhunate." *No mistaking it, and they must have noticed too, so she won't be hurt by my saying this. But I'll say no more. They mustn't learn she tried to save me the worst. Let 'em assume, under Ydwyr's guidance, that the news of her defection knocked me off my cam. Never mind gratitude or affection, lad; you'll need any hole card you can keep, and she may turn out to be one.* "You'll realize I . . . I am troubled. I'd be no more use here. They'll take off soon in any case. I'll go ahead and, well, think things over."

"Come," Cnif invited gently. "I will leave you alone."

He could not regret that his side was gaining an agent; but he could perceive, or believed he could perceive, Flandry's patriotic anguish. "Thanks," the human said, and grinned.

He started back along the trail. His boots thudded; occasionally a stone went clattering down the talus slope, or he slipped and nearly fell on a patch of ice. Lightlessness closed in, save where the solitary lance of his flashbeam bobbed and smoked through the vapors. He no longer noticed the cold, he was too busy planning his next move.

Cnif would naturally inform the rest that the Terran wasn't waiting for them. They wouldn't hasten after him on that account. Where could he go? Cnif would pour a stiffish drink for his distressed acquaintance. Curtained bunks were the most private places afforded by the bus. Flandry could be expected to seek his and sulk.

Light glowed yellow ahead from the black outline of the vehicle. It spilled on the Domrath's autumnal huts, their jerry-built frames already collapsing. Cnif's flat countenance peered anxiously from the forward section. Flandry doused his flash and went on all fours. Searching about, he found a rock that nicely fitted his hand. Rising, he approached in straightforward style and passed through the heatlock which tonight helped ward off cold.

The warmth inside struck with tropical force. Cnif waited, glass in hand as predicted, uncertain smile on mouth. "Here," he said with the blunt manners of a colonial, and thrust the booze at Flandry.

The man took it but set it on a shelf. "I thank you, courteous one," he replied in formal Eriau. "Would you drink with me? I need a companion."

"Why . . . I'm on duty . . . kh-h-h, yes. Nothing can hurt us here. I'll fetch myself one while you get out of

112

your overclothes." Cnif turned. In the cramped entry chamber, his tail brushed Flandry's waist and he stroked it lightly across the man, Merseia's gesture of comfort.

Quick! He must outmass you by twenty kilos!

Flandry leaped. His left arm circled Cnif's throat. His right hand brought the stone down where jaw met ear. They had taught him at the Academy that Merseians were weak there.

The blow crunched. Its impact nearly dislodged Flandry's grip on the rock. The other being choked, lurched, and swept his tail around. Flandry took that on the hip. Had it had more leverage and more room to develop its swing, it would have broken bones. As was, he lost his hold and was dashed to the floor. Breath whuffed out of him. He lay stunned and saw the enormous shape tower above.

But Cnif's counterattack had been sheer reflex. A moment the Merseian tottered, before he crumpled at knees and stomach. His fall boomed and quivered in the bus body. His weight pinned down the man's leg. When he could move again, Flandry had a short struggle to extricate himself.

He examined his victim. Though flesh bled freely—the same hemoglobin red as a man's—Cnif breathed. A horny lid, peeled back, uncovered the normal uniform jet of a Merseian eye, not the white rim that would have meant contraction. *Good.* Flandry stroked shakily the bald, serrated head. *I'd've hated to do you in, old chap. I would have if need be, but I'd've hated it.*

Hurry, you sentimental thimblewit! he scolded himself. *The others'll arrive shortly, and they tote guns.*

Still, after he had rolled Cnif out onto the soil, he found a blanket to wrap the Merseian in; and he left a portable glower going alongside.

Given that, the scientists would be in no serious trouble. They'd get chilled, wet, and hungry. Maybe a few would come down with sneezles and wheezles. But when Ydwyr didn't hear from them, he'd dispatch a flyer.

Flandry re-entered the bus. He'd watched how it was operated; besides, the basic design was copied from Technic civilization. The manual controls were awkward for human hands, the pilot seat more so for a human fundament. However, he could get by.

The engine purred. Acceleration thrust him backward. The bus lifted.

When high in the night, he stopped to ponder charts and plans. He dared not keep the stolen machine. On an otherwise electricityless and virtually metalless world, it could be detected almost as soon as a ship got aloft in search of it. He must land someplace, take out what he had in the way of stores, and send the bus off in whatever direction a wild goose would pick.

But where should he hide, and how long could he, on this winter-bound world?

Flandry reviewed what he had learned in the Merseian base and nodded to himself. Snowfall was moving south from the poles. The Ruadrath would be leaving the ocean, had probably commenced already. His hope of survival was not great, but his hope of raising hell was. He laid out a circuitous route to the coastlands west of Barrier Bay.

CHAPTER

XVI

When first they woke, the People had no names. He who was Rrinn ashore was an animal at the bottom of the sea.

Its changes were what roused him. Water pressure dropped with the level; lower temperatures meant a higher equilibrium concentration of dissolved oxygen, which affected the fairly shallow depths at which the People estivated; currents shifted, altering the local content of minerals raised from the ocean bed. Rrinn was aware of none of this. He knew only, without knowing that he knew, that the Little Death was past and he had come again to the Little Birth . . . though he would not be able to grasp these ideas for a while.

During a measureless time he lay in the ooze which lightly covered his submerged plateau. Alertness came by degrees, and hunger. He stirred. His gill flaps quivered, the sphincters behind them pumping for an ever more demanding bloodstream. When his strength was enough, he caught the sea with hands, webbed feet, and tail. He surged into motion.

Other long forms flitted around him. He sensed them primarily by the turbulence and taste they gave to the water. No sunlight penetrated here. Nevertheless vision picked them out as blurs of blackness. Illumination came from the dimly blue-glowing colonies of *aoao* (as it was called when the People had language) planted at the sides of the cage; it lured those creatures which dwelt always in the sea, and helped Wirrda's find their way to freedom.

Different packs had different means of guarding themselves during the Little Death, such as boulders rolled across crevices. Zennevirr's had even trained a clutch of finsnakes to stand sentry. Wirrda's slumbered in a cage—woven mesh between timbers—that nothing dangerous could enter. It had originally been built, and was annually repaired, in the spring when the People returned, still owning a limited ability to breathe air. That gave them energy to dive and do hard work below, living off the rede-

115

veloping gills an hour or two at a stretch. (Of course, not everyone labored. The majority chased down food for all.) After their lungs went completely inactive, they became torpid—besides, the sun burned so cruelly by then, the air was like dry fire—and they were glad to rest in a cool dark.

Now Rrinn's forebrain continued largely dormant, to preserve cells that otherwise would get insufficient oxygen. Instinct, reflex, and training steered him. He found one of the gates and undid it. Leaving it open, he swam forth and joined his fellows. They were browsing among the *aoao*, expropriating what undigested catch lay in those tentacles.

The supply was soon exhausted, and Wirrda's left in a widespread formation numbering about 200 individuals. Clues of current and flavor, perhaps subtler hints, guided them in a landward direction. Had it been clear day they would not have surfaced immediately; eyes must become reaccustomed by stages to the dazzle. But a thick sleet made broaching safe. That was fortunate, albeit common at this season. In their aquatic phase, the People fared best among the waves.

They found a school of—not exactly fish—and cooperated in a battue. Again and again Rrinn leaped, dived, drove himself by threshing tail and pistoning legs until he clapped hands on a scaly body and brought it to his fangs. He persisted after he was full, giving the extra catch to whatever infants he met. They had been born with teeth, last midwinter, able to eat any flesh their parents shredded for them; but years remained before they got the growth to join in a chase.

In fact, none of the People were ideally fitted for ocean life. Their remote ancestors, epochs ago, had occupied the continental shelf and were thus forced to contend with both floods and drought. The dual aerating system developed in response, as did the adaptation of departing the land to escape summer's heat. But being evolved more for walking than swimming—since two-thirds of their lives were spent ashore—they were only moderately efficient sea carnivores and "found" it was best to retire into estivation.

Rrinn had had that theory expounded to him by a Merseian paleontologist. He would remember it when his brain came entirely awake. At present he simply felt a wordless longing for the shallows. He associated them with food, frolic, and—and—

Snowing went on through days and nights. Wirrda's swam toward the mainland, irregularly, since they must hunt, but doggedly. Oftener and oftener they surfaced. Water felt increasingly less good in the gills, air increasingly less parching. After a while Rrinn actively noticed the sensuous fluidity along his fur, the roar and surge of great wrinkled foam-streaked gray waves, skirling winds and blown salt spindrift.

Snowing ended. Wirrda's broached to a night of hyaline clarity, where the very ocean was subdued. Overhead glittered uncountable stars. Rrinn floated on his back and gazed upward. The names of the brightest came to him. So did his own. He recalled that if he had lately passed a twin-peaked island, which he had, then he ought to swim in a direction that kept Ssarro Who Mounts Endless Guard over his right shoulder. Thus he would approach the feeding grounds with more precision than the currents granted. He headed himself accordingly, the rest followed, and he knew afresh that he was their leader.

Dawn broke lambent, but the People were no longer troubled by glare. They pressed forward eagerly in Rrinn's wake. By evening they saw the traces of land, a slight haze on the horizon, floating weeds and bits of wood, a wealth of life. That night they harried and were gluttonous among a million tiny phosphorescent bodies; radiance dripped from their jaws and swirled on every wave. Next morning they heard surf.

Rrinn identified this reef, that riptide, and swam toward the ness where Wirrda's always went ashore. At midafternoon the pack reached it.

North and south, eventually to cover half the globe, raged blizzards. Such water as fell on land, solid, did not return to the ocean; squeezed beneath the stupendous weight of later falls, it became glacier. Around the poles, the seas themselves were freezing, more territory for snow to accumulate on. In temperate climes their level dropped day by day, and the continental shelves reappeared in open air.

Rrinn would know this later. For the moment, he rejoiced to tread on ground again. Breakers roared, tumbled, and streamed among the low rocks; here and there churned ice floes. Swimming was not too dangerous, though. Winter tides were weak. And ahead, the shelf climbed, rugged and many-colored under a sparkling sky. Snow dappled its flanks, ice glistened where pools had been. The air was a riot of odors, salt, iodine, clean decomposition and fresh growth, and was crisp and windy and cool, cool.

Day after day the pack fattened itself, until blubber

sleeked out the bulges of ribs and muscles. The receding waters had left a rich stratum of dead plants and animals. In it sprouted last year's saprophyte seeds, salt and alcohol in their tissues to prevent freezing, and covered the rocks with ocherous and purple patches. Marine animals swarmed between; flying creatures shrieked and whirled above by the hundred thousand; big game wandered down from the interior to feed. Rrinn's males chipped hand axes to supplement their fangs; females prepared lariats of gut and sinew; beasts were caught and torn asunder.

Yet Wirrda's were ceasing to be only hunters. They crooned snatches of song, they trod bits of dance, they spoke haltingly. Many an individual would sit alone, hours on end, staring at sunset and stars while memory drifted up from the depths. And one day Rrinn, making his way through a whiteout, met a female who had kept close to him. They stopped in the wind-shrill blankness, the sea clashing at their feet, and looked eye into eye. She was sinuous and splendid. He exclaimed in delight, "But you are Cuwarra."

"And you are Rrinn," she cried. Male and wife, they came to each other's arms.

While ovulation was seasonal among the People, the erotic urge persisted throughout winter. Hence the young had fathers who helped care for them during their initial months of existence. That relationship was broken by the Little Death—older cubs were raised in casual communal fashion—but most couples stayed mated for life.

Working inland, Wirrda's encountered Brrao's and Hrrouf's. They did every year. The ferocious territoriality which the People had for their homes ashore did not extend to the shelf; packs simply made landfall at points convenient to their ultimate destinations. These three mingled cheerfully. Games were played, stories told, ceremonies put on, marriages arranged, joint hunts carried out. Meanwhile brains came wholly active, lungs reached full development, gills dried and stopped functioning.

Likewise did the shelflands. Theirs was a brief florescence, an aftermath of summer's furious fertility. Plants died off, animals moved away, pickings got lean. Rrinn thought about Wirrda's, high in the foothills beyond the tundra, where hot springs boiled and one river did not freeze. He mounted a rock and roared. Other males of his pack passed it on, and before long everyone was assembled beneath him. He said: "We will go home now."

Various youths and maidens complained, their courtships among Brrao's or Hrrouf's being unfinished. A few

118

hasty weddings were celebrated and numerous dates were made. (In the ringing cold of midwinter, the People traveled widely, by foot, sled, ski, and iceboat. Though hunting grounds were defended to the death, peaceful guests were welcomed. Certain packs got together at set times for trade fairs.) On the first calm day after his announcement, Rrinn led the exodus.

He did not start north at once. With full mentality regained, Wirrda's could use proper tools and weapons. The best were stored at Wirrda's—among the People, no real distinction existed among place names, possessives, and eponyms—but some had been left last spring at the accustomed site to aid this trek.

Rrinn's line of march brought his group onto the permanent littoral. It was a barren stretch of drifts. His Merseian acquaintances had shown him moving pictures of it during hot weather: flooded in spring, pullulating swamp in early summer, later baked dry and seamed with cracks. Now that the shelf was exhausted, large flesheaters were no longer crossing these white sastrugi to see what they could scoop out of the water. Rrinn pushed his folk unmercifully.

They did not mind the cold. Indeed, to them the land still was warmer than they preferred. Fur and blubber insulated them, the latter additionally a biological reserve. Theirs was a high homeothermic metabolism, with corresponding energy demands. The People needed a large intake of food. Rrinn took them over the wastelands because it would be slower and more exhausting to climb among the ice masses that choked Barrier Bay. Supplies could not be left closer to the shelf or the pack, witless on emergence, might ruin everything.

After three days' hard travel, a shimmer in the air ahead identified those piled bergs. Rrinn consulted Cuwarra. Females were supposed to be inferior, but he had learned to rely on her sense of direction. She pointed him with such accuracy that next morning, when he topped a hill, he looked straight across to his goal.

The building stood on another height, constructed of stone, a low shape whose sod roof bore a cap of white. Beyond it, in jagged shapes and fantastic rainbows, reached the bay. Northward wound the Golden River, frozen and snowed on and frozen again until it was no more than a blue-shadowed valley among the bluffs. The air was diamond-clear beneath azure heaven.

"Go!" shouted Rrinn exuberantly. Not just equipment, but smoked meat lay ahead. He cast himself on his belly

119

and tobogganed downslope. The pack whooped after. At the bottom they picked themselves up and ran. The snow crunched, without giving, under their feet.

But when they neared the building, its door opened. Rrinn stopped. Hissing dismay, he waved his followers back. The fur stood straight on him. An animal—

No, a Merseian. What was a Merseian doing in the cache house? They'd been shown around, it had been explained to them that the stuff kept there must never be disturbed, they'd agreed and—

Not a Merseian! Too erect. No tail. Face yellowish-brown where it was not covered with hair—

Snarling in the rage of territory violation, Rrinn gathered himself and plunged forward at the head of his warriors.

After dark the sky grew majestic with stars. But it was as if their light froze on the way down and shattered on the dimly seen ice of Talwin. A vast silence overlay the world; sound itself appeared to have died of cold. To Flandry, the breath in his nostrils felt liquid.

And this was the threshold of winter!

The Ruadrath were gathered before him in a semicircle ten or twelve deep. He saw them as a shadowy mass, occasionally a glitter when eyes caught stray luminance from the doorway where he stood. Rrinn, who confronted him directly, was clearer in his view.

Flandry was not too uncomfortable. The dryness of the air made its chill actually less hard to take than the higher temperatures of foggy autumn. From the bus he had lifted ample clothing, among divers other items, and bundled it around himself. Given a glower, the structure where he had taken refuge was cozy. Warmth radiated over his back.

(However, the glower's energy cells had gotten low in the three weeks that he waited. Likewise had his food. Not daring to tamper with the natives' stockpile, he had gone hunting—lots of guns and ammo in the bus—but, ignorant of local game, hadn't bagged much. And what he did get required supplementation from a dwindling stock of capsules. Nor could he find firewood. *If you don't convince this gentlebeing,* he told himself, *you're dead.*)

Rrinn said into a vocalizer from the cache house: "How foresaw you, new skyswimmer, that any among us would know Eriau?" The transponder turned his purring, trilling vocables into Merseian noises; but since he had never quite mastered a grammar and syntax based on a world-view unlike his own, the sentences emerged peculiar.

Flandry was used to that kind of situation. "Before leaving the Merseian base," he answered, "I studied what they had learned about these parts. They had plenty of material on you Ruadrath, among them you of Wirrda's. Mention was made of your depot and a map showed it. I knew you would arrive in due course." *I knew besides that it was unlikely the gatortails would check here for me, this close to their camp.* "Now you have been in contact with them since first they came—more than the Domrath, both because you are awake more and because they think more highly of you. Your interest in their works was often . . . depicted." (He had recalled that the winter folk used no alphabet, just mnemonic drawings and carvings.) "It was reasonable that a few would have learned Eriau, in order to discourse of matters which cannot be treated in any language of the Ruadrath. And in fact it was mentioned that this was true."

"S-s-s-s." Rrinn stroked his jaw. Fangs gleamed under stars and Milky Way. His breath did not smoke like a human's or Merseian's; to conserve interior heat, his respiratory system was protected by oils, not moisture, and water left him by excretion only. He shifted the harpoon he had taken from the weapon racks inside. Sheathed on the belt he had reacquired was a Merseian war knife. "Remains for you to tell us why you are here alone and in defiance of the word we made with the skyswimmers," he said.

Flandry considered him. Rrinn was a handsome creature. He wasn't tall, about 150 centimeters, say 65 kilos, but otter-supple. Otterlike too were the shape of body, the mahogany fur, the short arms. The head was more suggestive of a sea lion's, muzzle pointed, whiskered, and sharp-toothed, ears small and closeable, brain case bulging backward from a low forehead. The eyes were big and golden, with nictitating membranes, and there was no nose; breath went under the same opercula that protected the gills.

No Terran analogy ever holds very true. Those arms terminated in four-digited hands whose nails resembled claws. The stance was akin to Merseian, forward-leaning, counterbalanced by the long strong tail. The legs were similarly long and muscular, their wide-webbed feet serving as fins for swimming, snowshoes for walking. Speech was melodious but nothing that a man could reproduce without a vocalizer.

And the consciousness behind those eyes—Flandry picked his response with care.

"I knew you would be angered at my invading your cache house," he said. "I counted on your common sense to spare me when I made no resistance." *Well, I did have a blaster for backup.* "And you have seen that I harmed or took nothing. On the contrary, I make you gifts." *Generously supplied by the airbus.* "You understand I belong to a different race from the Merseians, even as you and the Domrath differ. Therefore, should I be bound by their word? No, let us instead seek a new word between Wirrda's and mine."

He pointed at the zenith. Rrinn's gaze followed. Flandry wondered if he was giving himself false reassurance in believing he saw on the Ruad that awe which any thoughtful sophont feels who lets his soul fall upward among the stars. *I'd better be right about him.*

"You have not been told the full tale, you of Wirrda's," he said into the night and their watchfulness. "I bring you tidings of menace."

CHAPTER
XVII

It was glorious to have company and be moving again.

His time hidden had not been totally a vacuum for Flandry. True, when he unloaded the bus—before sending it off to crash at sea, lest his enemies get a clue to him—he hadn't bothered with projection equipment, and therefore not with anything micro-recorded. Every erg in the accumulators must go to keeping him unfrozen. But there had been some full-size reading matter. Though the pilot's manual, the *Book of Virtues*, and a couple of scientific journals palled with repetition, the Dayr Ynvory epic and, especially, the volume about Talwin and how to survive on it did not. Moreover, he had found writing materials and a genuine human-style deck of cards.

But he dared not go far from his shelter; storms were too frequent and rough. He'd already spent most of his resources of contemplation while wired to the bunk in *Jake*. Besides, he was by nature active and sociable, traits which youth augmented. Initially, whenever he decided that reading one more paragraph would make his vitreous humor bubble, he tried sketching; but he soon concluded that his gifts in that direction fell a little short of Michelangelo. A more durable pastime was the composition of scurrilous limericks about assorted Merseians and superior officers of his own. A few ought to become interstellar classics, he thought demurely—if he got free to pass them on—which meant that he had a positive duty to survive. . . . And he invented elaborate new forms of solitaire, after which he devised ways to cheat at them.

The principal benefit of his exile was the chance to make plans. He developed them for every combination of contingencies that he could imagine. Yet he realized this must be kept within limits; unforeseen things were bound to pop up, and he couldn't risk becoming mentally rigid.

"All that thinking did raise my hopes," he told Rrinn.

"For us too?" the chief answered. He gave the man a contemplative look. "Skyswimmer, naught have we save your saying, that we should believe you intend our good."

123

"My existence is proof that the Merseians have not apprised you of everything. They never mentioned races in contention with them—did they?"

"No. When Ydwyr and others declared the world goes around the sun and the stars are suns themselves with worlds aspin in the same wise . . . that took years to catch. I did ask once, were more folk than theirs upon those worlds, and he said Merseia was friend to many. Further has he not related."

"Do you seize?" Flandry crowed. (He was getting the hang of Ruadrath idioms in Eriau. A man or Merseian would have phrased it, "Do you see?")

"S-s-s-s . . . Gifts have they given us, and in fairness have they dealt."

Why shouldn't they? Flandry gibed. *The scientists aren't about to antagonize their objects of research, and the Navy has no cause to. The reasons for being a tad less than candid about the interstellar political brew are quite simple. Imprimis, as this chap here is wise enough to understand, radically new information has to be assimilated slowly; too much at once would only confuse. Secundus, by its effect on religion and so forth, it tends to upset the cultures that Ydwyr's gang came to study.*

The fact is, friend Rrinn, the Merseians like and rather admire your people. Far more than the Domrath, you resemble them—or us, in the days of our pioneering.

But you must not be allowed to continue believing that.

"Among their folk and mine is a practice of keeping meat animals behind walls," he said. "Those beasts are treated well and fed richly . . . until time for slaughter."

Rrinn arched his back. His tail stood straight. He bared teeth and clapped hand to knife.

He had been walking with Flandry ahead of the group. It consisted chiefly of young, aged, and females. The hunters were scattered in small parties, seeking game. Some would not rejoin their families for days. When Rrinn stopped stiffened, unease could be seen on all the sleek red-brown bodies behind. The leader evidently felt he shouldn't let them come to a halt. He waved, a clawing gesture, and resumed his advance.

Flandry, who had modified a pair of Merseian snowshoes for himself, kept pace. Against the fact that he wasn't really built for this environment must be set his greater size. Furthermore, the going was currently easy.

Wirrda's were bound across the tundra that had been jungle in summer. Most years they visited the Merseian base, which wasn't far off their direct route, for sight-seeing, talk, and a handout. However, the practice wasn't invariable—it depended on factors like weather—and Flandry had made them sufficiently suspicious that on this occasion they jogged out of their way to avoid coming near the compound. Meanwhile he continued feeding their distrust.

The Hellkettles would have been visible except for being wrapped in storm. That part of horizon and sky was cut off by a vast blue-black curtain. Not for weeks or months would the atmosphere settle down to the clear, ever colder calm of full winter. But elsewhere the sky stood pale blue, with a few high cirrus clouds to catch sunlight.

This had dropped to considerably less than Terra gets. (In fact, the point of equal value had been passed in what meteorologically was early fall. Likewise, the lowest temperatures would come well after Talwin had gone through apastron, where insolation was about 0.45 Terran.) Flandry must nevertheless wear self-darkening goggles against its white refulgence; and, since he couldn't look near the sun disc, its dwindling angular diameter did not impinge on his senses.

His surroundings did. He had experienced winters elsewhere, but none like this.

Even on planets akin to Terra, that period is not devoid of life. On Talwin, where it occupied most of the long year, a separate ecology had developed for it.

The divorce was not absolute. Seas were less affected than land, and many shore-based animals that ate marine species neither hibernated nor estivated. Seeds and other remnants of a season contributed to the diet of those which did. The Merseians had hardly begun to comprehend the web of interactions—structural, chemical, bacteriological, none knew what more—between hot-weather and cold-weather forms. As an elementary example: No equivalent of evergreens existed; summer's wild growth would have strangled them; on the other hand, decaying in fall, it provided humus for winter vegetation.

The tundra reached in crisp dunes and a glimpse of wind-scoured frozen lake. But it was not empty. Black among the blue shadows, leaves thrust upward in clumps that only looked low and bushy; their stems often went down through meters of snow. The sooty colors absorbed sunlight with high efficiency, aided by reflection off the surface. In some, a part of that energy worked through molecular processes to liquefy water; others substituted organic compounds, such as alcohols, with lower freezing

125

points; for most, solidification of fluids was important to one stage or another of the life cycle.

North of the mountains, the glaciers were becoming too thick for plants. But south of them, and on the islands, vegetation flourished. Thus far it was sparse, and it would never approach the luxuriance of summer. Nonetheless it supported an animal population off which other animals lived reasonably well—including the Ruadrath.

Still, you could understand why they had such intense territorial jealousies. . . .

Flandry's breath steamed into air that lay cold on his cheeks; but within his garments he was sweating a trifle. The day was quiet enough for him to hear the *shuffle-shuffle* of his walking. He said carefully:

"Rrinn, I do not ask you to follow my counsel blind. Truth indeed is that I could be telling you untruth. What harm can it do, though, to consider ways by which you may prove or disprove my speech? Must you not as leader of Wirrda's attempt this? For think. If my folk and Merseia's are in conflict, maneuvering for position among the stars, then harbors are needed for the skyswimming craft. Not so? You have surely seen that not every Merseian is here to gather knowledge. Most come and go on errands that I tell you are scoutings and attacks on my folk.

"Now a warlike harbor needs defense. In preparation for the day the enemy discovers it, a day that will unfailingly come, it has to be made into more than a single small encampment. This whole world may have to be occupied, turned into a fortress." *What a casuist I am!* "Are you certain the Merseians have not been staring into your lives in order that they may know how easiest to overwhelm you?"

Rrinn growled back, "And am I certain your folk would leave us be?"

"You have but my speech," Flandry admitted, "wherefore you should ask of others."

"How? Shall I call Ydwyr in, show him you, and scratch for truth as to why he spoke nothing about your kindred?"

"N-n-no, I counsel otherwise. Then he need but kill me and give you any smooth saying he chooses. Best you get him to come to Wirrda's, yes, but without knowledge that I live. You can there draw him out in discourse and seize whether or not that which he tells runs together with that which you know from having traveled with me."

"S-s-s-s." Rrinn gripped his vocalizer as if it were a weapon. He was plainly troubled and unhappy; his revulsion at the idea of possibly being driven from his land gave him no peace. It lay in his chromosomes, the dread inherited from a million ancestors, to whom loss of hunting grounds had meant starvation in the barrens.

"We have the rest of the trek to think about what you should do," Flandry reassured him. *More accurately: for me to nudge you into thinking the scheme I hatched in the cache house is your own notion.*

I hope we do feel and reason enough alike that I can play tricks on you.

To himself: *Don't push too hard, Flandry. Take time to observe, to participate, to get* simpático *with them. Why, you might even figure out a way to make amends, if you survive.*

Chance changed the subject for him. A set of moving specks rounded a distant hill. Closer, they revealed themselves as a moose-sized shovel-tusked brute pursued by several Ruadrath. The hunters' yells split the air. Rrinn uttered a joyous howl and sped to help. Flandry was left floundering behind in spite of wanting to demonstrate his prowess. He saw Rrinn head off the great beast and engage it, knife and spear against its rushes, till the others caught up.

That evening there was feasting and merriment. The grace of dancers, the lilt of song and small drums, spoke to Flandry with an eloquence that went beyond language and species. He had admired Ruadrath art: the delicate carving on every implement, the elegant shapes of objects like sledges, bowls, and blubber lamps. Now tonight, sitting—bundled up—in one of the igloos that had been raised when the old females predicted a blizzard, he heard a story. Rrinn gave him a low-voiced running translation into Eriau. Awkward though that was, Flandry could identify the elements of style, dignity, and philosophy which informed a tale of heroic adventure. Afterward, meditating on it in his sleeping bag, he felt optimistic about his chances of manipulating Wirrda's.

Whether or not he could thereby wrest anything out of the Merseians was a question to be deferred if he wanted to get to sleep.

Ydwyr said quietly, "No, I do not believe you would be a traitress to your race. Is not the highest service you can render to help strike the Imperial chain off them?"

"What chain?" Djana retorted. "Where were the Emperor and his law when I tried to escape from the Black

127

Hole, fifteen years old, and my contractor caught me and turned me over to the Giggling Man for a lesson?"

Ydwyr reached out. His fingers passed through her locks, stroked her cheek, and rested on her shoulder for a minute. To save her garments—indoors being warm and she simply an alien there, her body neither desirable nor repulsive—she had taken to wearing just a pocketed kilt. The touch on her skin was at once firm and tender; its slight roughness emphasized the strength held in check behind. Love flowed through it, into her, and radiated back out from her until the bare small office was aglow, as golden sunsets can saturate the air of worlds like Terra.

Love? No, maybe not really. That's a typical sticky Anglic word. I remember, somebody told me, I think I remember . . . isn't it caritas *that God has for us mortals?*

Above the gray robe, above her, Ydwyr's countenance waited powerful and benign. *I mustn't call you God. But I can call you Father—to myself—can't I? In Eriau they say* rohadwann: *affection, loyalty, founded on respect and on my own honor.*

"Yes, I could better have spoken of burning out a cancer," he agreed. "The breakdown of legitimate authority into weakness or oppression—which are two aspects of the same thing, the change of Hands into Heads—is a late stage of the fatal disease." A human male would have tried to cuddle her and murmur consolations for memories that to this day could knot her guts and blur her eyesight. Then he would have gotten indignant if she didn't crawl into bed with him. Ydwyr continued challengingly: "You had the toughness to outlive your torment, at last to outwit the tormentors. Is not your duty to help those of your race to freedom who were denied your heritage?"

She dropped her gaze. Her fingers twisted together. "How? I mean, oh, you would overrun humanity . . . wouldn't you?"

"I thought you had learned the worth of propaganda," he reproached her. "Whatever the final result, you will see no enormous change; centuries of effort lie ahead. And the goal is liberation—of Merseians, yes, we make no bleat about our primary objective being anything else—but we welcome partners—and our endeavor is, ultimately, to impose Will on blind Nature and Chance."

Junior partners, she added to herself. *Well, is that necessarily bad?* She closed her eyes and saw a man who bore Nicky Flandry's face (descendant, maybe) striding in the van of an army which followed the Merseian Christ. He carried no exterior burden of venal superiors and bloodless colleagues, no interior load of nasty little guilts and doubts and mockeries; in his hand was the gigantic simplicity of a war knife, and he laughed as he strode. Beside him, she herself walked. Wind tossed her hair and roared in green boughs. They would never leave each other.

Nicky . . . dead . . . why? These people didn't kill him; no, not even those back yonder who wanted to wring him empty. They'd have been his friends if they could. The Empire wouldn't let them.

She looked again and found Ydwyr waiting. "Seeker," she said timidly, "this is too sudden for me. I mean, when *Qanryf* Morioch tells me I should, should, should become a spy for the Roidhunate—"

"You desire my advice," he finished. "You are always welcome to it."

"But how can I—"

He smiled. "That will depend on circumstances, my dear. After training, you would be placed where it was deemed you could be most useful. I am sure you realize the spectacular escapades of fiction are simply fiction. The major part of your life would be unremarkable—though I'm sure, with your qualifications, it would have a good share of glamour and luxury. For example, you might get a strategically placed Terran official to make you his mistress or his actual wife. Only at widely spaced intervals would you be in contact with your organization. The risks are less than those you habitually ran before coming here; the material rewards are considerable." He grew grave. "The real reward for you, my almost-daughter, will be the service itself. And knowing that your name will be in the Secret Prayers while the Vach Urdiolch endures."

"You do think I should?" she gulped.

"Yes," he said. "Those are less than half alive who have no purpose in life beyond themselves."

The intercom fluted. Ydwyr muttered annoyance and signaled it to shut up. It fluted twice more in rapid succession. He tensed. "Urgent call," he said, and switched on.

Cnif hu Vanden's image flicked into the screen. "To the *datholch*, homage," he said hurriedly. "He would not have been interrupted save that this requires his immediate attention. We have received a messenger from Seething Springs." Djana remembered hearing how fast a Ruad could travel when he had no family or goods to encumber him.

"Khr-r-r, they must be settling down there." Ydwyr's tailtip, peeking from beneath his robe, quivered, the single sign he gave of agitation. "What is their word?"

"He waits in the courtyard. Shall I give the *datholch* a direct line?"

"Do." Djana thought that a man would have asked for a briefing first. Men had not the Merseian boldness.

She couldn't follow the conversation between Ydwyr and the lutrine being who stood in the snow outside. The scientist used a vocalizer to speak the messenger's language. When he had blanked the screen, he sat for a long period, scowling, tailtip flogging the floor.

"Can I help?" Djana finally ventured to ask. "Or should I go?"

"*Shwai—*" He noticed her. "Khr-r-r." After pondering: "No, I can tell you now. You will soon hear in any case."

She contained herself. A Merseian aristocrat did not jitter. But her pulse thumped.

"A dispatch from the chief of that community," Ydwyr said. "Puzzling: the Ruadrath aren't in the habit of using ambiguous phrases, and the courier refuses to supplement what he has memorized. As nearly as I can discern, they have come on Dominic Flandry's frozen corpse."

Darkness crossed before her. Somehow she kept her feet.

"It has to be that," he went on, glowering at a wall. "The description fits a human, and what other human could it be? For some reason, instead of begetting wonder, this seems to have made them wary of us—as if their finding something we haven't told them about shows we may have designs on them. The chief demands I come explain."

He shrugged. "So be it. I would want to give the matter my personal attention regardless. The trouble must be smoothed out, the effects on their society minimized; at the same time, observation of those effects may teach us something new. I'll fly there tomorrow with—" He looked at her in surprise. "Why, Djana, you weep."

"I'm sorry," she said into her hands. The tears were salt on her tongue. "I can't help it."

"You knew he must be dead, the pure death to which you sent him."

"Yes, but—but—" She raised her face. "Take me along," she begged.

"*Haadoch?* No. Impossible. The Ruadrath would see you and—"

"And what?" She knelt before him and clutched at his lap. "I want to say goodbye. And . . . and give him . . . what I can of a Christian burial. Don't you understand, lord? He'll lie here alone forever."

"Let me think." Ydwyr sat motionless and expressionless while she tried to control her sobbing. At last he smiled, stroked her hair again, and told her, "You may."

She forgot to gesture gratitude. "Thank you, thank you," she said in ragged Anglic.

"It would not be right to forbid your giving your dead their due. Besides, frankly, I see where it can be of help, showing the Ruadrath a live human. I must plan what we should tell them, and you must have your part learned before morning. Can you do that?"

"Certainly." She lifted her chin. "Afterward, yes, I will work for Merseia."

"Give no rash promises; yet I hope you will join our cause. That fugitive talent you have for making others want what you want—did you use it on me?" Ydwyr blocked her denial with a lifted palm. "Hold. I realize you'd attempt no mind-intrusion consciously. But unconsciously— *Khraich,* I don't suppose it makes any difference in this case. Go to your quarters, Djana daughter. Get some rest. I will be summoning you in a few hours."

CHAPTER
XVIII

Where their ranges overlapped, Domrath and Ruadrath normally had no particular relationship. The former tended to regard the latter as supernatural; the latter, having had chances to examine hibernator dens, looked more matter-of-factly on the former. Most Domrath left Ruadrath things strictly undisturbed—after trespassing groups had been decimated in their sleep—whereas the Ruadrath found no utility in the primitive Domrath artifacts. The majority of their own societies were chalcolithic.

But around Seething Springs—Ktha-g-klek, Wirrda's—a pattern of mutuality had developed. Its origins were lost in myth. Ydwyr had speculated that once an unusual sequence of weather caused the pack to arrive here while the tribe was still awake. The Ruadrath allowed summertime use of their sturdy buildings, fine tools, and intricate decorations, provided that the users were careful and left abundant food, hides, fabrics, and similar payment. To the Domrath, this had become the keystone of their religion. The Ruadrath had found ceremonial objects and deduced as much. It made Wirrda's a proud band.

Flandry discovered he could play on that as readily as on territorial instinct. You may admit the skyswimmers can do tricks you can't. Nevertheless, when you are accustomed to being a god, you will resent their not having told you about the real situation in heaven.

Rrinn and his councilors were soon persuaded to carry out the human's suggestion: Send an obscurely worded message, which Flandry helped compose. Keep back the fact that he was alive. Have nearly everyone go to the hinterland during the time the Merseians were expected; they could do nothing against firearms, and a youngster might happen to give the show away.

Thus the village lay silent when the airbus appeared.

Domed with the snow that paved the spiderweb passages between them, buildings looked dwarfed. The winter sky was so huge and blue, the treeless winter horizon so remote. Steam from the springs and geysers dazzled Flan-

132

dry when he glimpsed it, ungoggled; for a minute residual light-spots hid the whitened mass of Mt. Thunderbelow and the glacier gleam on the Hellkettle peaks. Fast condensing out, vapors no longer smoked above the Neverfreeze River. But its rushing rang loud in today's icy quiet.

A lookout yelled, *"Trreeann!"* Flandry had learned that call. He peered upward and southward, located the glinting speck, and sprang into the house where he was to hide.

Its door had been left open, the entrance covered by a leather curtain—an ordinary practice which should not draw any Merseian heed. Within, among the strewn furs and stacked utensils of a prosperous owner, sunbeams straggled past cracks in the shutters to pick out of dimness the arsenal Flandry had taken from the vehicle he stole. He carried two handguns, blaster and stunner, plus a war knife, extra ammunition, and energy charges. That was about the practical limit. The rest Wirrda's could inherit, maybe.

The house fronted on the central plaza. Directly opposite stood Rrinn's, where the meeting was to take place. Thus the Ruad could step out and beckon the human to make a dramatic appearance if and when needed. (*That's what Rrinn thinks.*) Through a minute hole in the curtain, Flandry saw the nine males who remained. They were armed. Ydwyr had never given them guns, which would have affected their culture too radically for his liking. But those bronze swords and tomahawks could do ample damage.

Rrinn spoke grimly into his short-range transceiver. Flandry knew the words he did not understand: "Set down at the edge of our village, next to the tannery. Enter afoot and weaponless."

Ydwyr should obey. It's either that or stop xenologizing this pack. And why should he fear? He'll leave a few lads in the bus, monitoring by radio, ready to bail him out of any trouble.

That's what Ydwyr thinks.

Some minutes later the Merseians showed up. They numbered four. Despite their muffling coldsuits, Flandry recognized the boss and three who had been on that previous trip to this country—how many years of weeks ago—

A small shape, made smaller yet by the tyrannosaurian bulks preceding, entered his field of view. He caught his breath. It was not really too surprising that Djana had also come. But after so much time, her delicate features and gold hair struck through the fishbowl helmet like a blow.

The Ruadrath gave brief greeting and took the newcomers inside. Rrinn entered last, drawing his own door curtain. The plaza lay bare.

Now.

Flandry's hands shook. Sweat sprang forth on his skin, beneath which the heart thuttered. Soon he might be dead. And how piercingly marvelous the universe was!

The sweat began freezing on his unprotected face. The beard he had grown, after his last application of inhibitor lost effect, was stiff with ice. In a few more of Talwin's short days, he would have used his final dietary capsule. Eating native food, minus practically every vitamin and two essential amino acids, was a scurvy way to die. Being shot was at least quick, whether by a Merseian or by himself if capture got imminent.

He stood a while, breathing slowly of the keen air, willing his pulse rate down, mentally reciting the formulas which drugs had conditioned him to associate with calm. The Academy could train you well if you had the foresight and persistence to cooperate. Loose and cool, he slipped outdoors. Thereafter he was too busy to be afraid.

A quick run around the house, lest somebody glance out of Rrinn's and see him . . . a wall-hugging dash down the glistering streets, snow crunching under his boots . . . a peek around the corner of the outlying tannery . . . yes, the bus sat where it was supposed to be, a long streamlined box with sun-shimmer off the windows.

If those inside spotted him and called an alarm, that was that. *The odds say nobody'll happen to be mooning in this direction. You know what liars those odds are.* He drew his stunner, crouched, and reached the main heatlock in about two seconds.

Flattened against the side, he waited. Nothing occurred, except that his cheekbone touched the bus. Pain seared. He pulled free, leaving skin stuck fast to metal. Wiping away tears with a gloved hand, he set his teeth and reached for the outer valve.

It wasn't locked. Why should it be, particularly when the Merseians might want to pass through in a hurry? He glided into the chamber. Again he waited. No sound. He cracked the inner valve and leaned into the entry. It was deserted.

They'll have somebody in front, by the controls and communication gear. And probably someone in the main room, but let's go forward for openers. He oozed down the short passage.

A Merseian, who must have heard a noise or felt a

134

breath of cold air—in this fantastic oily-smelling warmth —loomed into the control cabin doorway. Flandry fired. A purple light ray flashed, guiding the soundless hammer-blow of a supersonic beam. The big form had not toppled, unconscious, when Flandry was there. Another greenskin was turning from the pilot console. *"Gwy—"* He didn't say further before he thudded to the deck.

Whirling, Flandry sped toward the rear. The saloon windows gave on the remaining three sides of the world; an observation dome showed everything else. Two more Merseians occupied that section. One was starting off to investigate. His gun was out, but Flandry, who entered shooting, dropped him. His partner, handicapped by being in the turret, was easier yet, and sagged into his seat with no great fuss.

Not pausing, the human hurried forward. Voices drifted from a speaker: Merseian basso, Ruadrath purr and trill, the former using vocalizers to create the latter. He verified that, to avoid distraction, there had been no transmission from the bus.

Then he allowed himself to sit down, gasp, and feel dizzy. *I carried it off. I really did.*

Well, the advantage of surprise—and he was only past the beginning. Trickier steps remained. He rose and searched about. When he had what he needed, he returned to his prisoners. They wouldn't wake soon, but why take chances? One was Cnif. Flandry grinned with half a mouth. "Am I to make a hobby of collecting you?"

Having dragged the Merseians together, he wired them to bunks—"Thanks, Djana"—and gagged them. On the way back, he appropriated a vocalizer and a pair of sound recorders. In the pilot cabin he stopped the input from Rrinn's house.

Now for the gristly part. Though he'd rehearsed a lot, that wasn't sufficient without proper apparatus. Over and over he went through his lines, playing them back, read-justing the transducer, fiddling with speed and tone con-trols. (Between tests, he listened to the conference. The plan called for Rrinn to draw palaver out at length, pump-ing Ydwyr's delegation. But the old xenologist was not naive—seemed, in fact, to be one of the wiliest characters Flandry had ever collided with—and might at any time do something unforeseeable. Words continued, however.) Fi-nally the human had what he guessed was the best voice imitation he could produce under the circumstances.

He set his recorders near the pickup for long-range radio. Impulses flew across 300 white kilometers. A machine said: "The *datholch* Ydwyr calls Naval Operations. Priority for emergency. Respond!"

"The *datholch's* call is acknowleged by *Mei* Chwioch, Vach Hallen," answered a loudspeaker.

Flandry touched the same On button. "Record this order. Replay to your superiors at once. My impression was false. The Terran Flandry is alive. He is here at Seething Springs, at the point of death from malnutrition and exposure. The attempt must be made to save him, for he appears to have used some new and fiendishly effective technique of subversion on the Ruadrath, and we will need to interrogate him about that. Medical supplies appropriate to his species ought to be in the scoutboat that was taken. Time would be lost in ransacking it. Have it flown here immediately."

"The *datholch's* command is heard and shall be relayed. Does anyone know how to operate the vessel?"

Flandry turned on his second machine. It went "Kh-h-hr," his all-purpose response. In this context, he hoped, it would pass for a rasping of scorn. *A pilot who can't figure that out in five minutes, when we use the same basic design, should be broken down to galley swabber and set to peeling electrons.* He made his first recorder say: "Land in the open circle at the center of the village. We have him in a house adjacent. Hurry! Now I must return to the Ruadrath and repair what damage I can. Do not interrupt me until the boat is down. Signing off. Honor to the God, the Race, and the Roidhun!"

He heard the response, stopped sending, and tuned the conference back in. It sounded as if fur was about to fly.

So, better not dawdle here. Besides, *Jake* should arrive in minutes if his scheme worked.

If.

Well, they wouldn't be intimately familiar with Ydwyr's speech in the Navy section . . . aside from high-ranking officers like Morioch, who might be bypassed for the sake of speed, seeing as how Merseia encouraged initiative on the part of juniors . . . or if a senior did get a replay, he might not notice anything odd, or if he did he might put it down to a sore throat . . . or, or, or—

Flandry scrambled back into the overclothes he had shucked while working. He stuffed some cord in a pocket. A chronodial said close to an hour had fled. It stopped when he fired a blaster bolt at the main radio transmitter. On his way out, he sabotaged the engine too, by lifting a shield plate and shooting up the computer that regulated the grav projectors. He hoped not to kill anyone in his escape, but he didn't want them sharing the news before he was long gone. Of course, if he must kill he would, and lose no sleep afterward, if there was an afterward.

The air stung his injury. He loped over creaking snow to Rrinn's house. Closer, he moved cautiously, and stopped at the entrance to squeeze his eyes shut while raising his goggles. Charging indoors without dark-adapted pupils would be sheer tomfoolishness. Also dickfoolishness, harryfoolishness, and— Stunner in right hand, blaster in left, he pushed by the curtain. It rustled stiffly into place behind him.

Merseians and Ruadrath swiveled about where they tail-sat. They were at the far end of the single chamber, their parties on opposite daises. A fleeting part of Flandry noticed how vivid the murals were at their backs and regretted that he was about to lose the friendship of the artist.

Djana cried out. Rrinn hissed. Ydwyr uttered a sentence in no language the man had heard before. Several males of either species started off the platforms. Flandry brandished his blaster and shouted in Eriau: "Stay where you are! This thing's set to wide beam! I can cook the lot of you in two shots!"

Tensed and snarling, they returned to their places. Djana remained standing, reaching toward Flandry, mouth open and working but no sound coming forth. Ydwyr snapped into his vocalizer. Rrinn snapped back. The Terran could guess:

"What is this treachery?"

"Indeed we had him alive; yet I know not what he would seize."

He interrupted: "I regret I must stun you. No harm will be done, aside from possible headaches when you awaken. If anyone tries to attack me, I'll blast him. The blast will likely kill others. Rrinn, I give you a few breaths to tell your followers this."

"You wouldn't!" Djana protested wildly.

"Not to you, sweetheart," Flandry said, while Ruadrath words spat around him. "Come over here by me."

She gulped, clenched fists, straightened and regarded him squarely. "No."

"Huh?"

"I don't turn my coat like you."

"I wasn't aware I had." Flandry glared at Ydwyr. "What have you done to her?"

"I showed her truth," the Merseian answered. He had regained his calm. "What do you expect to accomplish?"

"You'll see," Flandry told him. To Rrinn: "Are you finished?"

"*Ssnaga.*" No matter the Ruad was of another species; you could not mistake unutterable hatred.

Flandry sighed. "I grieve. We traveled well together. Good hunting be yours for always."

The guide ray struck and struck. The Ruadrath scuttled for shelter, but found nothing high enough. The Merseians took their medicine with iron dignity. After a minute, none among them was conscious save Ydwyr and Djana.

"Now." Flandry tossed her the loop of cord. "Tie his wrists at his back, run his tail up there and make it fast, then pass down the end and hobble him."

"No!" she shrieked.

"Girl," said the gaunt, sun-darkened, wounded visage with the frost in its beard, "more's involved than my life, and I'm fond of living to start with. I need a hostage. I'd prefer not to drag him. If I have to, though, I'll knock you both out."

"Obey," Ydwyr told her. He considered Flandry. "Well done," he said. "What is the next stage of your plan?"

"No comment," the man replied. "I don't wish to be discourteous, but what you don't know you can't arrange to counteract."

"Correct. It becomes clear that your prior achievements were no result of luck. My compliments, Dominic Flandry."

"I think the *datholch.* —Get cracking, woman!"

Djana's gaze went bewildered between them. She struggled not to cry.

Her job of tying was less than expert; but Flandry, who supervised, felt Ydwyr couldn't work out of it fast. When she was through, he beckoned her to him. "I want our playmate beyond your reach," he said. Looking down into the blue eyes, he smiled. There was no immediate need now to aim a gun. He laid both hands on her waist. "And I want you in my reach."

"Nicky," she whispered, "you don't know what you're doing. Please, please listen."

"Later." A sonic boom made pots jump on a shelf. In spite of the dictatorship he had clamped down on himself, something leaped likewise in Flandry. "Hoy, that's my ticket home."

He peered past the curtain. Yes, *Giacobini-Zinner,* dear needle-nosed *Jake,* bulleting groundward, hovering, settling in a whirl of kicked-up snow. . . . Wait! Far off in the sky whence she'd come—

Flandry groaned. It looked like another spacecraft. Morioch or somebody had played cautious and sent an escort.

Well, he'd reckoned with that possibility. A Comet had the legs over most other types, if not all; and in an atmosphere, especially Talwin's—

The lock opened. The gangway extruded. A Merseian appeared, presumably a physician since he carried the medikit he must have ferreted out on his way here. He wasn't wearing an electric coldsuit, only Navy issue winter clothes. Suddenly it was comical beyond belief to see him stand there, glancing puzzled around, with his tail in a special stocking. Flandry had seldom worked harder than to hold back whoops and yell, in his best unaided imitation of a Merseian voice: "Come here! On the double! Your pilot too!"

"Pilot—"

"Hurry!"

The doctor called into the boat. Both Merseians descended and started across the ground. Flandry stood bowstring-tense, squinting out the slit between jamb and curtain, back to the captives he already had, out, in, out, in. If somebody got suspicious or somebody shouted a warning before the newcomers were in stunbeam range, he'd have to blast them dead and attempt a dash for the vessel.

They entered. He sapped them.

Recovering the medikit, he waved his gun. "Let's go, Ydwyr." He hesitated. "Djana, you can stay if you want."

"No," the girl answered, nigh too weakly to hear. "I'll come."

"Best not," Ydwyr counseled. "The danger is considerable. We deal with a desperate being."

"Maybe I can help you," Djana said.

"Your help would be to Merseia," Ydwyr reproved her.

Flandry pounced. "That's what you are to him, girl," he exclaimed in Anglic. "A tool for his damned planet." In Eriau: "Move, you!"

The girl shook her head blindly. It wasn't clear which of them she meant. Forlorn, she trudged out behind the tall nonhuman figure, in front of the man's weapon.

High and distant, little more in the naked eye than a glint, the enemy ship held her position. Magniscreens would reveal that three left the house for the boat—but not their species, Flandry hoped. Just three sent out to fetch something. . . . The gangway clattered to boots.

"Aft," Flandry directed. "Sorry," he said when they

were at the bunks, and stunned Ydwyr. He used the cord to secure his captive and urged Djana forward. Her lips, her whole slight body trembled.

"What will you do?" she pleaded.

"Try to escape," Flandry said. "You mean there's a different game going?"

She sank into the seat beside his control chair. He buckled her in, more as a precaution against impulsive behavior than against a failure of interior grav, and assumed his own place. She stared blankly at him. "You don't understand," she kept repeating. "He's good, he's wise, you're making such a terrible mistake, please don't."

"You want me brainscrubbed, then?"

"I don't know, I don't know. Let me alone!"

Flandry forgot her while he checked the indicators. Everything seemed in order, no deterioration, no vandalism, no boobytraps. He brought the engine murmurous to life. The gangway retracted, the airlock shut. *Goodbye, Talwin. Goodbye, existence? We'll see.* He tickled the console. The skill had not left his fingers. *Jake* floated aloft. The village receded, the geysers, the mountains, he was skyborne.

The outercom blinked and buzzed. Flandry ignored it till he was lined out northward. The other spacecraft swung about and swooped after him. Several kilometers off, she proved to be a corvette, no capital ship but one that could eat a scoutboat for breakfast. Flandry accepted her call.

"*Saniau* to Terran vessel. Where are you bound and why?"

"Terran vessel, and she is a Terran vessel, to *Saniau.* Listen with both ears. Dominic Flandry speaks. That's right, the very same Dominic Flandry who. I'm going home. The *datholch* Ydwyr, Vach Urdiolch, nephew to the most exalted Roidhun and so forth, is my guest. If you don't believe me, check the native town and try to find him. When he recovers from a slight indisposition, I can give you a visual. Shoot me down and he goes too."

Pause.

"If you speak truth, Dominic Flandry, do you imagine the *datholch* would trade honor for years?"

"No. I do imagine you'll save him if you possibly can."

"Correct. You will be overhauled, grappled, and boarded. If the *datholch* has been harmed, woe betide you."

"First you have to do the overhauling. Second you have to convince me that any woe you can think of betides me

140

worse than what does already. I suggest you check with the *qanryf* before you get reckless. Meanwhile," and in Anglic, "cheerio." Flandry cut the circuit.

At his velocity, he had crossed the Hellkettle Mountains. The northlands stretched vast and drear beneath, gleaming ice, glittering snow, blots that were blizzards. He cast about with his instruments for a really huge storm. There was sure to be one somewhere, this time of year . . . yes!

A wall of murk towered from earth to high heaven. Before he had pierced it, Flandry felt the thrust and heard the scream of hurricane-force winds. When he was inside, blackness and chaos had him.

A corvette would not go into such a tempest. Nothing except a weathership had any business in one; others could flit above or around readily enough. But a small spaceboat with a first-class pilot—a pilot who had begun his career in aircraft and aerial combat—could live in the fury. And detectors, straining from outside, would lose her.

Flandry lost himself in the battle to keep alive.

Half an hour later, he broke free and shot into space.

Talwin rolled enormous in his screens. Halfway down from either pole coruscated winter's whiteness; the cloud-marbled blue of seas between icecaps looked black by contrast. Flandry waved. "Goodbye," he said anew. "Good luck."

Meters shouted to his eyes of patrol ships waiting for him. You didn't normally risk hyperdrive this near a planet or a sun. Matter density was too great, as was the chance of gravitation desynchronizing your quantum jumps. The immediate scene was scarcely normal. Flandry's hands danced.

Switchover to secondary state in so strong a field made the hull ring. Screens changed to the faster-than-light optical compensation mode. Talwin was gone and Siekh dwindling among the stars. The air droned. The deck shivered.

After minutes, a beep drew Flandry's attention to a telltale. "Well," he said, "one skipper's decided to be brave and copy us. He got away with it, too, and locked onto our 'wake.' His wouldn't register that steady a bearing otherwise. We're faster, but I'm afraid we won't shake him before he's served as a guide to others who can outpace us."

Djana stirred. She had sat mute—lost, he thought when he could spare her a thought—while they ran the polar storm. Her face turned to him beneath its heavy coif of hair. "Have you any hope?" she asked tonelessly.

He punched for navigational data. "A stern chase is a long chase," he said, "and I've heard about a pulsar not many parsecs off. It may help us shed our importunate colleagues."

She made no response, simply looked back out at space. Either she didn't know how dangerous a pulsar was, or she didn't care.

CHAPTER
XIX

Once a blue giant sun had burned, 50,000 times more luminous than yet-unborn Sol. It lasted for a bare few million years; then the hydrogen fuel necessary to stay on the main sequence was gone. The star collapsed. In the unimaginable violence of a supernova, momentarily blazing to equal an entire galaxy, it went out.

Such energies did not soon bleed away. For ages the blown-off upper layers formed a nebula of lacy loveliness around the core, which shone less white-hot than X-ray hot. Eventually the gases dissipated, a part of them to make new suns and planets. The globe that remained continued shrinking under its own weight until density reached tons per cubic centimeter and spin was measured in seconds. Feebler and feebler did it shine, white dwarf, black dwarf, neutron star—

Compressed down near the ultimate that nature's law permitted, the atoms (if they could still be called that) went into their final transitions. Photons spurted forth, were pumped through the weirdly distorted space-time within and around the core, at last won freedom to flee at light speed. Strangely regular were those bursts, though slowly their frequencies, amplitudes, and rate declined back toward extinction—dying gasps.

Pulsar breath.

Djana stared as if hypnotized into the forward screen. Tiny but waxing among the stars went that red blink . . . blink . . . blink. She did not recall having ever seen a sight more lonely. The cabin's warmth and glow made blacker the emptiness outside; engine throb and ventilator murmur deepened the eternal silence of those infinite spaces.

She laid a hand on Flandry's arm. "Nicky—"

"Quiet." His eyes never left the board before him; his fingers walked back and forth across computer keys.

"Nicky, we can die any minute, and you've said hardly a word to me."

"Stop bothering me or we will for sure die."

She retreated into her chair. *Be strong, be strong.*

He had bound her in place for most of the hours during which the boat flew. She didn't resent that; he couldn't trust her, and he must clean himself and snatch some sleep. Afterward he brought sandwiches to his captives—she might have slipped a drug into his—and released her. But at once he was nailed to instrument and calculations. He showed no sign of feeling the wishes she thrust at him; his will to liberty overrode them.

Now he crouched above the pilot panel. He'd not been able to cut his hair; the mane denied shaven countenance, prim coverall, machine-controlling hands, and declared him a male animal who hunted.

And was hunted. Four Merseian ships bayed on his heels. He'd told her about them before he went to rest, estimating they would close the gap in 25 light-years. From Siekh to the pulsar was 17.

Blink . . . blink . . . blink . . . once in 1.3275 second.

Numbers emerged on a plate set into the console. Flandry nodded. He took the robotic helm. Stars wheeled with his shift of course.

In time he said, maybe to himself: "Yes. They're decelerating. They don't dare come in this fast."

"What?" Djana whispered.

"The pursuit. They spot us aiming nearly straight on for that lighthouse. Get too close—easy to do at hyperspeed—and the gravity gradient will pluck you apart. Why share the risk we have to take? If we don't make it, Ydwyr will've been more expendable than a whole ship and crew. If we do survive, they can catch us later."

And match phase, and lay alongside, and force a way in to rescue Ydwyr . . . and her . . . but Nicky, Nicky they would haul off to burn his brain out.

Should it matter? I'll be sorry, we both will be sorry for you, but Merseia—

He turned his head. His grin and gray eyes broke across her like morning. "That's what they think," he said.

I only care because you're a man, the one man in all this wasteland, and do I care for any man? Only my body does, my sinful body. She struggled to raise Ydwyr's face.

Flandry leaned over and cupped her chin in his right hand. "I'm sorry to've been rude," he smiled. "Sorrier to play games with your life. I should have insisted you stay on Talwin. When you wanted to come, with everything else on my mind I sort of assumed you'd decided you preferred freedom."

"I was free," she said frantically. "I followed my master."

"Odd juxtaposition, that." A buzzer sounded. "'Scuse, I got work. We go primary in half a shake. I've programed the autopilot, but in conditions this tricky I want to ride herd on it."

"Primary?" Dismay washed through her. "They'll catch you right away!" *That's good. Isn't it?*

The engine note changed. Star images vanished till the screens readapted. At true speed, limited by light's, the boat plunged on. Power chanted abaft the cabin; she was changing her kinetic velocity at maximum thrust.

Blink . . . blink . . . blink . . . The blood-colored beacon glowed ever brighter. Yet Djana could look directly into it, and she did not find any disc. Stars frosted the night around. Which way was the Empire?

Flandry had given himself back to the machines. Twice he made a manual adjustment.

After minutes wherein Djana begged God to restore Merseian courage to her, the noise and vibration stopped. Head full of it, she didn't instantly recognize its departure. Then she bit her tongue to keep from imploring a word.

When Flandry gave her one, she started shivering.

He spoke calmly, as if these were the lost days when they two had fared after treasure. "We're in the slot, near's I can determine. Let's relax and give the universe our job for a bit."

"Wh-wh-what are we doing?"

"We're falling free, in a hyperbolic orbit around the pulsar. The Merseians aren't. They're distributing themselves to cover the region. They can't venture as close as us. The potential of so monstrous a mass in so small a volume, you see; differential forces would wreck their ships. The boat's less affected, being of smaller dimensions. With the help of the interior field—the same that gives us artificial gravity and counteracts acceleration pressure—she ought to stay in one piece. The Merseians doubtless figure to wait till we kick in our hyperdrive again, and resume the chivvy."

"But what're we getting?" Blink . . . blink . . . blink . . . Had his winter exile driven him crazy?

"We'll pass through the fringes of a heavily warped chunk of space. The mass concentration deforms it. If the core got much denser, light itself couldn't break loose. We won't be under any such extreme condition, but I don't expect they can track us around periastron. Our emission will be too scattered; radar beams will curve off at silly angles. The Merseians can compute roughly where and when we'll return to flatter space, but until we do—" Flandry had unharnessed himself while he talked. Rising, he stretched prodigiously, muscle by muscle. "Ā propos Merseians, let's go check on old Ydwyr."

Djana fumbled with her own buckles. "I, I, I *don't* track you, Nicky," she stammered. "What do we . . . you gain more than time? Why did you take us aboard?"

"As to your first question, the answer's a smidge technical. As to the second, well, Ydwyr's the reason we've come this far. Without him, we'd've been in a missile barrage." Flandry walked around behind her chair. "Here, let me assist."

"You! You're not unfastening me!"

"No, I'm not, am I?" he said dreamily. Leaning over, he nuzzled her where throat met shoulder. The kiss that followed brought a breathless giddiness which had not quite faded when he led the way aft.

Ydwyr sat patient on a bunk. Prior to sleeping, Flandry had welded a short length of light cable to the frame, the other end around an ankle, and untied the rope. It wasn't a harsh confinement. In fact, the man would have to keep wits and gun ready when negotiating this passage.

"Have you been listening to our conversation?" he asked. "I left the intercom on."

"You are thanked for your courtesy," Ydwyr replied, "but I could not follow the Anglic."

"Oh!" Djana's hand went to her mouth. "I forgot—"

"And I," Flandry admitted. "We Terrans tend to assume every educated being will know our official language —by definition—and of course it isn't so. Well, I can tell you."

"I believe I have deduced it," Ydwyr said. "You are swinging free, dangerously but concealingly near the pulsar. From the relativistic region you will launch your courier torpedoes, strapped together and hyperdrives operating simultaneously. What with distortion effects, you hope my folk will mistake the impulses for this boat's and give chase. If your decoy lures them as far as a light-year off, you will be outside their hyperwave detection range and can embark on a roundabout homeward voyage. The sheer size of space will make it unlikely that they, backtracking, will pick up your vibrations."

"Right," Flandry said admiringly. "You're a sharp rascal. I look forward to some amusing chit-chat."

"If your scheme succeeds." Ydwyr made a salute of respect. "If not, and if we are taken alive, you are under my protection."

Gladness burst in Djana. *My men can be friends!*

"You are kind," said Flandry with a bow. He turned to the girl. "How about making us a pot of tea?" he said in Anglic.

"Tea?" she asked, astonished.

"He likes it. Let's be hospitable. Put the galley intercom on—low—and you can hear us talk."

Flandry spoke lightly, but she felt an underlining of his last sentence and all at once her joy froze. *Though why, why?* "Would . . . the *datholch* . . . accept tea?" she asked in Eriau.

"You are thanked." Ydwyr spoke casually, more interested in the man. Djana went forward like an automaton. The voices trailed her:

"I am less kind, Dominic Flandry, than I am concerned to keep an audacious and resourceful entity functional."

"For a servant?"

"Khraich, we cannot well send you home, can we? I—"

Djana made a production of closing the galley door. It cut off the words. Fingers unsteady, she turned the intercom switch.

"—sorry. You mean well by your standards, I suppose, Ydwyr. But I have this archaic prejudice for freedom over even the nicest slavery. Like the sort you fastened on that poor girl."

"A reconditioning. It improved her both physically and mentally."

No! He might be speaking of an animal!

"She does seem more, hm, balanced. It's just a seeming, however, as long as you keep that father-image hood over her eyes."

"Hr-r-r, you have heard of Aycharaych's techniques, then?"

"Aycharaych? Who? N-n-no . . . I'll check with Captain Abrams . . . Damn! I should have played along with you, shouldn't I? All right, I fumbled that one, after you dropped it right into my paws. Getting back to Djana, the father fixation is unmistakable to any careful outside observer."

"What else would you have me do? She came, an unwitting agent who had acquired knowledge which must not get back to Terra. She showed potentialities. Instead of killing her out of hand, we could try to develop them. Death is always available. Besides, depth-psychological work on a human intrigued me. Later, when that peculiar

147

gift for sometimes imposing her desires on other minds appeared, we saw what a prize we had. My duty became to make sure of her."

"So to win her trust, you warned her to warn me?"

"Yes. About—in honesty between us, Dominic Flandry —a fictitious danger. No orders had come for your removal; I was welcome to keep you. But the chance to clinch it with her was worth more."

Anglic: "No! I'll—be—especially—damned."

"You are not angry, I hope."

"N-n-no. That'd be unsporting, wouldn't it?" Anglic: "The more so when it caused me to break from my cell with a hell of a yell far sooner than I'd expected to."

"Believe me, I did not wish to sacrifice you. I did not want to be involved in that wretched business at all. Honor compelled me. But I begrudged every minute away from my Talwinian research."

Djana knelt on the deck and wept.

Blink . . . blink . . . blink . . . furnace glare spearing from the screens. The hull groaned and shuddered with stresses. Fighting them, the interior field set air ashake in a wild thin singing. Often, looking down a passage, you thought you saw it ripple; and perhaps it did, sliding through some acute bend in space. From time to time hideous nauseas twisted you, and your mind grew blurred. Sunward was only the alternation of night and red. Starward were no constellations nor points of light, nothing but rainbow blotches and smears.

Djana helped Flandry put the courier torpedoes, which he had programed under normal conditions, on the launch rack. When they were outside, he must don a spacesuit and go couple them. He was gone a long while and came back white and shaken. "Done," was everything he would tell her.

They sought the conn. He sat down, she on his lap, and they held each other through the nightmare hours. "You're real," she kept babbling. "You're real."

And the strangeness faded. Quietness, solidity, stars returned one by one. A haggard Flandry pored over instruments whose readings again made sense, about which he could again think clearly.

"Receding hyperwakes," he breathed. "Our stunt worked. Soon's we stop registering them—First, though, we turn our systems off."

"Why?" she asked from her seat to which she had returned, and from her weariness.

148

"I can't tell how many the ships are. Space is still somewhat kinky and—well, they may have left one posted for insurance. The moment we pass a threshold value of the metric, there'll be no mistaking our radiation, infrared from the hull, neutrinos from the powerplant, that kind of junk. Unless we douse the sources."

"Whatever you want, darling."

Weightlessness was like stepping off a cliff and dropping without end. Cabin dark, the pulsar flash on one side and stars on the other crowded near in dreadful glory. Nothing remained save the faintest accumulator-powered susurrus of forced ventilation; and the cold crept inward.

"Hold me," Djana beseeched into the blindness. "Warm me."

A pencil-thin flashbeam from Flandry's hand slipped along the console. Back-scattered light limned him, a shadow. Silence lengthened and lengthened until:

"Uh-oh. They're smart as I feared. Grav waves. Somebody under primary acceleration. Has to be a ship of theirs."

Son of Man, help us.

At the boat's high kinetic velocity, the pulsar shrank and dimmed while they watched.

"Radar touch," Flandry reported tonelessly.

"Th-they've caught us?"

"M-m-m, they may assume we're a bit of cosmic débris. You can't check out every blip on your scope. . . . Oof! They're applying a new vector. Wish I dared use the computer. It looks to me as if they're maneuvering for an intercept with us, but I'd need math to make sure."

"If they are?" *The abstractness of it, that's half the horror. A reading, an equation, and me closed off from touching you, even seeing you. We're not us, we're objects. Like being already dead—no, that's not right, Jesus promised we'll live. He did.*

"They aren't necessarily. No beam's latched onto us. I suspect they've been casting about more or less at random. We registered strong enough to rate a closer look, but they lost and haven't refound us. Interplanetary space is bigger than most people imagine. So they may as well direct themselves according to the orbit this whatsit seemed to have, in hopes of checking us out at shorter range."

"Will they?"

"I don't know. If we're caught . . . well, I suppose we should eschew a last-ditch stand. How would one dig a ditch in vacuum? We can surrender, hope Ydwyr can save us and another chance'll come to worm out." His voice in the dark was not as calm as he evidently wished.

"You'd trust Ydwyr?" lashed from her.

His beam stepped across the dials. "Closing in fast," he said. "Radar sweep's bound to pick us up soon. We *may* show as an interstellar asteroid, but considering the probability of a natural passage at any given time—" She heard and felt his despair. "Sorry, sweetheart. We gave 'em a good try, didn't we?"

The image might have sprung to her physical vision, shark shape across the Milky Way, man's great foes black-clad at the guns. She reached out to the stars of heaven. "God have mercy," she cried with her whole being. "Oh, send them back where they belong!"

Blink . . . blink . . . blink.

The light ray danced. Where it touched, meters turned into pools beneath those suns that crowded the screens. "Ho-o-old," Flandry murmured. "One minute . . . They're receding!" exploded from him. "Judas priest, they, they must've decided the blip didn't mean anything!"

"They're going?" she heard herself blurt. "They are?"

"Yes. They are. Can't've felt too strongly about that stray indication they got. . . . Whoo! They've gone hyper! Already! Aimed back toward Siekh, seems like. And the —here, we can use our circuits again, lemme activate the secondary-wave receivers first—yes, yes, four indications, our couriers, their other three ships, right on the verge of detectability, headed out—Djana, we did it! Judas priest!"

"Not Judas, dear," she said in worship. "Jesus."

"Anybody you like." Flandry turned on the fluoros. Joy torrented from him. "You yourself—your wonderful, wonderful self—" Weight. Warm hearty gusts of air. Flandry was doing a fandango around the cabin. "We can take off ourselves inside an hour. Go a long way round for safety's sake—but at the end, home!" He surged to embrace her. "And never mind Ydwyr," he warbled. "We're going to celebrate the whole way back!"

CHAPTER

XX

Standing in the cramped, thrumming space between bulkheads, beyond reach of him who sat chained, the Terran said: "You appreciate that the whole truth about what happened would embarrass me. I want your solemn promise you'll support my account and drop no hint concerning Wayland."

"Why should I agree?" the Merseian asked blandly.

"Because if you don't," Djana told him—venom seethed in each word—"I'll have the pleasure of killing you."

"No, no, spare the dramatics," Flandry said. "Especially since he too considers an oath under duress is worthless. Ydwyr, the pilot's data list various planets where I could let you off. You can survive. A few have intelligent natives to study. Their main drawback is that no one has found any particular reason to revisit them, so you may have a slight problem in publishing your findings. But if you don't mind, I don't."

"Is that not a threat?" the prisoner rumbled.

"No more than your threat to expose my, ah, sideline financial interests. Talwin's bound to lose its military value whatever becomes of you or me. Suppose I throw in that I'll do what I can to help keep your scientific station alive. Under the circumstances, does that bargain sound fair?"

"Done!" Ydwyr said. He swore to the terms by the formulas of honor. Afterward he extended a hand. "And for your part, let us shake on it."

Flandry did. Djana watched, gripping a stunner. "You're not figuring to turn him loose now, are you?" she demanded.

"No, I'm afraid that can't be included in the deal," Flandry said. "Unless you'll give me your parole, Ydwyr."

The girl looked hurt and puzzled, then relieved when the Merseian answered:

"I will not. You are too competent. My duty is to kill you if I can." He smiled. "With that made clear, would you like a game of chess?"

151

Mining continued here and there in the system to which Irumclaw belonged. Hence small human colonies persisted, with mostly floating populations that weren't given to inconvenient curiosity or to gossiping with officialdom about what they might have seen.

Jake put briefly down in a spaceport on the fourth world out. It was a spot of shabbiness set in the middle of an immense rusty desert. The atmosphere was not breathable, and barely thick enough to blow dust clouds into a purple sky. A gangtube reached forth to connect airlock with airdome. Flandry escorted Djana to the exit.

"You'll be through soon?" she asked wistfully. For a moment the small slender form in the modest gown, the fine-boned features, eyes like blue lakes, lips slightly parted and aquiver, made him forget what had passed between them and think of her as a child. He had always been a sucker for little girls.

"Soon's I can," he answered. "Probably under a week. But do lie doggo till you hear from me. It's essential we report jointly to Leon Ammon. Those credits you brought with you ought to stretch. Check the general message office daily. When my 'gram comes, go ahead and shoot him word to have somebody fetch you. I'll be standing by." He kissed her more lightly than had been his wont. "Cheers, partner."

Her response was feverish. "Partners, yes!" she said afterward, in an unsteady tone. A tear broke away. She turned and walked fast from the airlock. Flandry went back to the conn and requested immediate clearance for takeoff.

Above his gorgeous tunic, Admiral Julius wore the least memorable face that Flandry had ever seen. "Well!" he said. "Quite a story, Lieutenant. Quite a story."

"Yes, sir," Flandry responded. He stood beside Ydwyr, who tail-sat at ease—if with ill-concealed contempt for the ornate office—in a robe that had been hastily improvised for him. His winter garb being unsuitable for shipboard, he had traveled nude and debarked thus on Irumclaw; and you *don't* receive princes of the blood in their nakedness.

"Ah . . . indeed." Julius shuffled some papers on his desk. "As I understand your—your supervisor's verbal redaction of what you told him—you are writing a report in proper form, are you not?—as I understand it . . . well, why don't you tell me yourself?"

"Yes, sir. Cruising on my assigned route, I detected the 'wake' of a larger vessel. As per standing orders, I moved

152

closer to establish identification. She was an unmistakable Merseian warcraft. My orders gave me discretion, as the admiral knows, whether to report the sighting in person with no further ado or attempt finding out more. Rightly or wrongly, I decided on the second course. Chances were against another encounter and we might be left with no further leads. I dropped back and sent a courier, which apparently never got here. My report's going to recommend tightening inspection procedures.

"Well, I shadowed the Merseian at the limits of detectability—for me—which I thought would keep my smaller vessel outside her sensor range. But we entered the range of another ship, a picket, that spotted me, closed in, and made capture. I was brought to the planet Talwin, where the Merseians turned out to have an advanced base. After miscellaneous brouhaha, I escaped via a pulsar, taking this dignitary along for a hostage."

"Um-m-m, ah." Julius squinted at Ydwyr. "An awkward affair, yes. They were technically within their rights, building that base, weren't they? But they had no right to hold an Imperial vessel and an Imperial officer . . . in a region free by treaty. Um." It was blatant that he shrank from being caught in the middle of a diplomatic crisis.

"If it please the admiral," Flandry said, "I speak Eriau. The *datholch* and I have held some long conversations. Without attempting to make policy or anything, sir—I know I'm forbidden to—I did feel free to suggest a few thoughts. Would the admiral care to have me interpret?" It had turned out the base's linguistic computer was on the fritz and nobody knew how to fix it.

"Ah . . . yes. Certainly. Tell his, ah, his highness we consider him a guest of the Imperium. We will try to, ah, show him every courtesy and arrange for his speedy transportation home."

"He's physicked anxious to shoot you off and bury this whole affair deep," Flandry informed Ydwyr. "We can do anything we choose with him."

"You will proceed according to plan, then?" the scientist inquired. His expression was composed, but Flandry had learned how to recognize a sardonic twinkle in a Merseian eye.

"*Kraich,* not exactly a plan. The fact of Talwin cannot be hidden. GHQ will see a report and assign an investigator. What we want is to save face all around. You've been offered a ride back, as I guessed you would be. Accept it for the earliest possible moment. When you reach Talwin, get Morioch to evacuate his ships and personnel. The planet will be of no further use for intelligence operations anyway; your government's sure to order them shut down. If our Navy team finds nothing going on but peaceful xenological research, they'll gloss over what signs are left of extracurricular activity, and nothing will likely be said on either side about this contretemps that you and I were involved in."

"I have already assented to your making these proposals in my name. Proceed."

Flandry did, in more tactful language. Julius beamed. If his command was instrumental in halting an undesirable Merseian project, word would circulate among the higher-ups. It would influence promotions, rotation to more promising worlds, yes, yes, no matter how discreetly the affair was handled. *A discretion which'll result in nobody's caring to notice whatever loose ends dangle out of my story,* Flandry thought.

"Excellent, Lieutenant!" Julius said. "My precise idea! Tell his highness I'll make prompt arrangements."

Ydwyr said gravely: "I fear the research will not long endure. With no bonus of military advantage—"

"I told you I'd do my best for you," Flandry answered, "and I've been mulling a scheme. Didn't want to advance it till I was sure we could write our own playbill, but now I am. See, I'll put on an indignation act for you. Maybe your folk should not have detained me; still, you are of the Vach Urdiolch and my cavalier treatment of you was an insult to the Race. Seeing that he's avid to please, you've decided to milk old Julius. You'll let yourself be mollified if he'll strongly urge that the Imperium help support the scientific work which, officially, will have been Merseia's reason for being on Talwin in the first place."

The big green body tautened. "Is that possible?"

"I imagine so. We'll have to keep watch on Talwin from here on anyway, lest your Navy sneak back. It needn't be from scoutboats, though. A few subsidized students or the like, doing their graduate thesis work, are quite as good and a lot cheaper. And . . . with us sharing the costs, I daresay you can find money at home to carry on."

A small renaissance of Terran science? Hardly. Academic hackwork. Oh, I suppose I can indulge in the hope.

"In the name of the God." Ydwyr stared before him for a length of time that made Julius shift and harrumph. At last he gripped both of Flandry's hands and said, "From that beginning, our two people working together, what may someday come?"

Nothing much, except, I do dare hope, a slight rein-

forcement of the reasons for our hanging onto this frontier. Those Merseians may keep us reminded who's always ready to fill any available vacuum. "The *datholch* bears a noble dream."

"What's this?" Julius puffed. "What are you two doing?"

"Sir, I'm afraid we've hit a rock or two," Flandry said.

"Really? How long will this take? I have a dinner engagement."

"Maybe we can settle the difficulty before then, sir. May I be seated? I thank the admiral. I'll do my best, sir. Got my personal affairs to handle too."

"No doubt." Julius regarded the young man calculatingly. "I am told you've applied for furlough and reassignment."

"Yes, sir. I figure those months on Talwin more than completed my tour of duty here. No reflection on this fine command, but I am supposed to specialize along other lines. And I believe I may have an inheritance coming. Rich uncle on a colonial planet wasn't doing too well, last I heard. I'd like to go collect my share before they decide a 'missing in action' report on me authorizes them to divvy up the cash elsewhere."

"Yes. I see. I'll approve your application, Lieutenant, and recommend you for promotion." ("If you bail me fast out of this mess" was understood.) "Let's get busy. What is the problem you mentioned?"

The room above Door 666 was unchanged, a less tasteful place to be than the commandant's and a considerably more dangerous one. The Gorzunian guard stirred no muscle; but light gleamed off a scimitar thrust under his gun belt. Behind the desk, Leon Ammon sweated and squeaked and never took his needle gaze off Flandry. Djana gave him head-high defiance in return; her fists, though, kept clenching and unclenching on her lap, and she had moved her chair into direct contact with the officer's.

He himself talked merrily, ramblingly, and on the whole, discounting a few reticences, truthfully. At the end he said, "I'll accept my fee—in small bills, remember—with unparalleled grace."

"You sure kept me waiting," Ammon hedged. "Cost me extra, trying to find out what'd happened and recruit somebody else. I ought to charge the cost to your payment. Right?"

"The delay wasn't my fault. You should have given your agent better protection, or remuneration such that she had

155

no incentive to visit persons to whom she'd not been introduced." Flandry buffed fingernails on tunic and regarded them critically. "You have what you contracted for, a report on Wayland, favorable at that."

"But you said the secret's been spilled. The Merseians—"

"My friend Ydwyr the Seeker assures me he'll keep silence. The rest of whatever personnel on Talwin have heard about the Mimirian System will shortly be dispersed. In any event, why should they mention a thing that can help Terra? Oh, rumors may float around, but you only need five or ten years' concealment and communication is poor enough to guarantee you that." Flandry reached for a cigarette. Having shed the addiction in these past months, he was enjoying its return. "Admittedly," he said, "if I release Ydwyr from his promise, he may well chance to pass this interesting item—complete with coordinates—on to the captain of whatever Imperial ship arrives to look his camp over."

Ammon barked a laugh. "I expected a response from you, Dominic. You're a sharp-edge boy." He stroked his chins. "You thought about maybe resigning your commission? I could use a sharp-edge boy. You know I pay good. Right?"

"I'll know that when I've counted the bundle," Flandry said. He inhaled the tobacco into lighting and rolled smoke around his palate.

The gross bulk wallowed forward in its chair. The bald countenance hardened. "What about the agent who got to Djana?" Ammon demanded. "And what about her?"

"Ah, yes," Flandry answered. "You owe her a tidy bit, you realize."

"What? After she—"

"After she, having been trapped because of your misguided sense of economy, obtained for you the information that you've been infiltrated, yes, dear heart, you are in her debt." Flandry smiled like a tiger. "Naturally, I didn't mention the incident in my official report. I can always put my corps on the trail of those Merseian agents without compromising myself, as for example by sending an anonymous tip. However, I felt you might prefer to deal with them yourself. Among other inducements, they've probably also corrupted members of your esteemed competitor associations. You might well obtain facts useful in your business relationships. I'm confident your interrogators are persuasive."

"They are," Ammon said. *"Who is the spy?"*

Djana started to speak. Flandry forestalled her with a

156

reminding gesture. "The information is the property of this young lady. She's willing to negotiate terms for its transfer. I am her agent."

Sweat studded Ammon's visage. "Pay her—when she tried to sell me out?"

"My client Djana will be leaving Irumclaw by the first available ship. Incidentally, I'm booking passage on the same one. She needs funds for her ticket, plus a reasonable stake at her destination, whatever it may be."

Ammon spat a vileness. The Gorzunian sensed rage and bunched his shaggy body for attack.

Flandry streamed smoke out his nose. "As her agent," he went mildly on, "I've taken the normal precautions to assure that any actions to her detriment will prove unprofitable. You may as well relax and enjoy this, Leon. It'll be expensive at best, and the rate goes up if you use too much of our valuable time. I repeat, you can take an adequate return out of the hide of that master spy, when you've purchased the name."

Ammon waved his goon back. Hatred thickening his voice, he settled down to dicker.

No liners plied this far out. The *Cha-Rina* was a tramp freighter with a few extra accommodations modifiable for various races. She offered little in the way of luxuries. Flandry and Djana brought along what pleasant items they were able to find in Old Town's stores. No other humans were aboard, and apart from the skipper, who spent her free hours in the composition of a caterwauling sonata, the Cynthian crew spoke scant Anglic. So they had privacy.

Their first few days of travel were pure hedonism. To sleep out the nightwatch, lie abed till the clock said noon, loaf about and eat, drink, read, watch a projected show, play handball, listen to music, make love in comfort—before everything else, to have no dangers and no duties—seemed ample splendor. But the ship approached Ysabeau, itself richly endowed with cities and a transfer point for everywhere else in the bustling impersonal vastness of the Empire; and they had said nothing yet about the future.

"Captain's dinner," Flandry decreed. While he stood over the cook, and ended preparing most of the delicacies himself, Djana ornamented their cabin with what cloths and furs she could find. Thereafter she spent a long while ornamenting herself. For dress she chose the thinnest, fluffiest blue gown she owned. Flandry returned, slipped into red-and-gold mufti, and popped the cork on the first champagne bottle.

They dined, and drank, and chatted, and laughed through a couple of hours. He pretended not to see that she was forcing her mirth. The moment when he must notice came soon enough.

He poured brandy, lounged back, sniffed and sipped. "Aahh! Almost as tasty as you, my love."

She regarded him across the tiny, white-clothed table. Behind her a viewscreen gave on crystal dark and a magnificence of stars. The ship shivered and hummed ever so faintly, the air was fragrant with odors from the cleared-away dishes, and with the perfume she had chosen. Her great eyes fell to rest and he could not dip his own from them.

"You use that word a lot," she said, quiet-voiced. "Love."

"Appropriate, isn't it?" Uneasiness tugged at him.

"Is it? What do you intend to do, Nicky?"

"Why . . . make a dummy trip to 'claim my inheritance.' Not that anybody'd check on me especially, but it's an excuse to play tourist. When my leave's up, I report to Terra, no less, for the next assignment. I daresay somebody in a lofty echelon has gotten word about the Talwin affair and wants to talk to me—which won't hurt the old career a bit, eh?"

"You've told me that before. You know it's not what I meant. Why have you never said anything about us?"

He reached for a cigarette while taking a fresh swallow of brandy. "I have, I have," he countered, smiling hard. "With a substantial sum in your purse, you should do well if you make the investments I suggested. They'll buy you a peaceful life on a congenial planet; or, if you prefer to shoot for larger stakes, they'll get you entry into at least the cellars of the *haut monde*."

She bit her lip. "I've been dreading this," she said.

"Hey? Uh, you may've had a trifle more than optimum to drink, Djana. I'll ring for coffee."

"No." She clenched fingers about the stem of her glass, raised it and tossed off the contents in a gulp. Setting it down: "Yes," she said, "I did kind of guzzle tonight. On purpose. You see, I had to form the habit of not thinking past any time when I was feeling good, because knowing a bad time was sure to come, I'd spoil the good time. A . . . an inhibition. Ydwyr taught me how to order my inhibitions out of my way, but I didn't want to use any stunt of that bastard's—"

158

"He's not a bad bastard. I've grown positively fond of him."

"—and besides, I wanted to pull every trick in my bag on you, and for that I needed to be happy, really happy. Well, tonight's my last chance. Oh, I suppose I could stay around a while—"

"I wouldn't advise it," Flandry said in haste. He'd been looking forward to searching for variety in the fleshpots of the Empire. "I'll be too peripatetic."

Djana shoved her glass toward him. He poured, a clear gurgle in a silence where, through the humming, he could hear her breathe.

"Uh-huh," she said. "I had to know tonight. That's why I got a touch looped, to help me ask." She lifted the glass. Her gaze stayed on his while she drank. Stars made a frosty coronet for her hair. When she had finished, she was not flushed. "I'll speak straight," she said. "I thought . . . we made a good pair, Nicky, didn't we, once things got straightened out? . . . I thought it wouldn't hurt to ask if you'd like to keep on. No, wait, I don't have any notions about me as an agent. But I could be there whenever you got back."

Well, let's get it over with. Flandry laid a hand on one of hers. "You honor me beyond my worth, dear," he said. "It isn't possible—"

"I supposed not." Had Ydwyr taught her that instant steely calm? "You'd never forget what I've been."

"I assure you, I'm no prude. But—"

"I mean my turnings, my treasons. . . . Oh, let's forget I spoke, Nicky, darling. It was just a hope. I'll be fine. Let's enjoy our evening together; and maybe, you know, maybe sometime we'll meet again."

The thought slashed through him. He sat straight with a muttered exclamation. *Why didn't that occur to me before?*

She stared. "Is something wrong?"

He ran angles and aspects through his head, chuckled gleefully at the result, and squeezed her fingers. "Contrariwise," he said, "I've hit on a sort of answer. If you're interested."

"What? I— What *is* it?"

"Well," he said, "you brushed off the idea of yourself in my line of work as a fantasy, but weren't you too quick? You've proven you're tough and smart, not to mention beautiful and charming. On top of that, there's this practically unique wild talent of yours. And Ydwyr wouldn't be hard to convince you've zigzagged back to him. Our Navy

159

Intelligence will jump for joy to have you, after I pass word along the channels open to me. We'd see each other often, I daresay, perhaps now and then we'd work together. . . . why, even if they get you into the Roidhunate as a double agent—"

He stopped. Horror confronted him.

"What . . . what's the matter?" he faltered.

Her lips moved several times before she could speak. Her eyes stayed dry and had gone pale, as if a flame had passed behind them. There was no hue at all in her face.

"You too," she got out.

"Huh? I don't—"

She checked him by lifting a hand. "Everybody," she said, "as far back as I can remember. Ending with Ydwyr, and now you."

"What in cosmos?"

"Using me." Her tone was flat, not loud in the least. She stared past him. "You know," she said, "the funny part is, I wanted to be used. I wanted to give, serve, help, belong to somebody. . . . But you only saw a tool. A thing. Every one of you."

"Djana, I give you my word of honor—"

"Honor?" She shook her head, slowly. "It's a strange feeling," she told her God, in a voice turned high and puzzled, like that of a child who cannot understand, "to learn, once and forever, that there's no one who cares. Not even You."

She squared her shoulders. "Well, I'll manage."

Her look focused on Flandry, who sat helpless and gaping. "As for you," she said levelly, "I guess I can't stop you from having almost any woman who comes by. But I'll wish this, that you never get the one you really want."

He thought little of her remark, then. "You're overwrought," he said, hoping sharpness would work. "Drunk. Hysterical."

"Whatever you want," she said wearily. "Please go away."

He left, and arranged for a doss elsewhere. Next morn-watch the ship landed on Ysabeau. Djana walked down the gangway without saying goodbye to Flandry. He watched her, shrugged, sighed—*Women! The aliens among us!*—and sauntered alone toward the shuttle into town, where he could properly celebrate his victory.